"Pregnancy agrees with you, Marissa. You look even more beautiful each day."

"Where is all thi

He got up and w
toward her. He p

"I don't just want
to be in your life, Marissa.

He held her snugly. "This feels so right to me," he whispered. "I want you to know that you're not alone. We can get through anything you're facing. We can do it together."

She leaned back to look up at him, studying his expression.

Something stirred within Griffin, and he smiled then.

"What?" Marissa asked.

He pulled her close and kissed her lips. When her tongue met his, he felt shivers of desire race through him.

Marissa matched him kiss for kiss, and in no time he felt the heat they'd generated that fateful night.

Books by Jacquelin Thomas

Harlequin Kimani Romance

The Pastor's Woman
Teach Me Tonight
Chocolate Goodies
You and I
Case of Desire
Five Star Attraction
Five Star Temptation
Legal Attraction

JACQUELIN THOMAS

is an award-winning, bestselling author with more than thirty-five books in print. When she is not writing, she is busy working toward a degree in psychology. Jacquelin and her family live in North Carolina.

Legal Attraction

Jacquelin Thomas

HARLEQUIN®

entertain, enrich, inspire™

Jacquelin Thomas is acknowledged as the author of this work.

Recycling programs
for this product may
not exist in your area.

ISBN-13: 978-0-373-86281-8

LEGAL ATTRACTION

For questions and comments about the quality of this book, please contact us at CustomerService@Harlequin.com.

www.Harlequin.com

Printed in U.S.A.

Dear Reader,

Lawyers, a high-profile case, romance and secrets… what could make a better story? In the third and final book of the Laws of Love series, you will bear witness to the love affair between Griffin Jackson and Marissa, the youngest daughter of Jacob Hamilton.

In *Legal Attraction,* Marissa discovers a long-kept family secret which threatens to tear her world apart. Just when she feels that her life will never be the same, she and Griffin find that the love they share cannot be ignored. As the evidence is presented, it is my hope that you will agree with the verdict that there is no escaping true love.

Thanks for your support!

Sincerely,

Jacquelin

Chapter 1

"Harper, why are you just staring at me like that?" Marissa Hamilton asked, regarding her cousin with somber curiosity. She had never seen him look so stricken.

Something is wrong.

He turned and closed her office door so they would not be disturbed. "I just found out something that I think you should know, Marissa."

"What is this about, Harper?"

He looked as if he were weighing the question.

"Harper …" she prompted.

"I guess there's no way to say this except to just say it," Harper muttered after a moment. He took a deep breath and exhaled slowly before saying, "Marissa, this is about my dad, your mother and you."

Confused, Marissa frowned. "You aren't making

any sense, Harper. What does Uncle Frank have to do with me and my mother?"

"Dad and Aunt Jeanette had an affair," Harper said in a low voice.

"Harper, have you lost your mind? H-how—" Marissa stammered in bewilderment. "How could you let something like that come out of your mouth?"

There was a pensive shimmer in the shadow of Harper's eyes. "Marissa, you have to know that I wouldn't come to you with a lie this painful if it wasn't true." His gaze was almost pleading. "I wouldn't have said anything to you otherwise."

"It's not true," Marissa insisted. She felt her composure was under attack and she suddenly wanted to escape Harper's disturbing presence. "I don't believe a word of this, but even if it were true, it has nothing to do with me."

"Marissa…" He paused a moment before adding, "Don't you get it? You may not be my cousin. We may be siblings." Tears formed in his eyes. "This is so messed up."

She swallowed hard, trying to digest what Harper had just told her. It could not possibly be true. It had to be a lie.

"My dad and your mother had an affair twenty-seven years ago," he told her. Harper swiped at his eyes.

Marissa shook her head in denial. "I don't believe any of this, Harper. My mother would never cheat on my father and definitely not with his brother. Where did you hear this?"

"Does it really matter?" Harper asked.

She glared at him. "I don't get how you could believe

anything like this about your dad and my mother of all people. None of this is true, Harper," Marissa stated firmly. "Whoever is spouting this lie is just trying to destroy our family."

"Azure would not do anything to hurt this family," he blurted. "She got this from an anonymous source and immediately came to me with it. Marissa, I didn't want to believe it at first either."

Harper's new wife, Azure, was a magazine writer and as such had numerous "sources." Marissa folded her arms across her chest. "Harper, why are you so convinced that it's true?"

"I know that my dad had an affair with your mother because I confronted him. He admitted that it was true."

Marissa felt as if she had been punched in the stomach. She was about to be sick. Dizziness threatened to overtake her, causing her to sway.

Harper reached for her when it looked as if Marissa was about to faint.

She steadied herself. "I'm fine. I just need some time alone."

"Marissa, I'm so sorry, but I thought you should know the truth."

"Please…I just need to be alone right now. I'll be okay," she assured him.

When Harper left her office, Marissa navigated slowly over to the plush sofa in her office and sank down, grateful for its welcoming embrace.

She tearfully surveyed her office, the rich mahogany furnishings, the Oriental rug—she knew every inch of the law firm located in the prewar building in Rittenhouse Square in the historic city of Philadelphia. This place had been her second home since the day she was born. That familiarity suddenly seemed to diminish by Harper's declaration that Jacob Hamilton Jr. might not be her biological father.

Jacob and her mother, Jeanette, raised five children together: Jacob III, Anthony, Marcus, Jillian and her. Marissa knew that her parents loved and respected each other. There was just no way that her prim and proper mother would have an affair with her brother-in-law.

The Hamiltons were a very close-knit family. She and her siblings were all attorneys and worked in the family firm. Frank and three of his sons, Harper, Shawn and Benjamin, were also attorneys working at Hamilton, Hamilton and Clark. Only Frank and Vanessa's son Nelson decided to go against tradition and pursued a career in acting instead.

"I need to get out of here," Marissa whispered.

She paused to let her assistant know that she was stepping out for a half hour or so, and would be back in time for her next meeting.

Marissa strolled out of the building and walked down the street to a tree-filled park. She found an empty bench and sat down. In about an hour, local residents and employees gathering for lunch would overrun the park. The October weather was still nice enough to sit outside in and enjoy eating with friends and family.

A small group of children playing nearby caught her attention. One little girl fell down and began to cry. A man rushed over and scooped her up into his arms.

Marissa felt her own eyes water at the sight of a father soothing his daughter and wiping away her tears. Her father…Jacob had done the same for her so many times when she was younger. He had always made her feel safe and loved.

She knew deep down that Harper never would have come to her if he did not have a reason to believe his hideous revelation was true. She also knew that Azure would not reveal the secret, but someone out there was spreading this rumor.

Marissa feared that if the information ever became public, it would have a devastating impact on her family and the firm.

Griffin Jackson was usually in his office by seven-thirty on weekdays. He liked coming in early just to spend some time reflecting over his day without any distractions. Griffin was usually the first one to arrive in the mornings and the last one to leave Hamilton, Hamilton and Clark in the evenings.

The now deceased Jacob Hamilton Sr. and Albert Clark had founded the family-owned law firm in 1960. Albert Clark was still active, although eighty years old. He shared leadership of the company with Jacob Jr. and Frank.

Griffin had interned at Hamilton, Hamilton and Clark while in law school and had been offered a permanent position by Albert Clark, who had taken the young man under his wing. Griffin had met Albert Clark when the esteemed attorney gave a lecture at the University of Pennsylvania Law School. The day after graduation, Griffin had started his career with the firm, and he had been with the company for five years.

The hours were long, leaving little time for socialization, but as far as Griffin was concerned, this was a dream come true for him and he would make the necessary sacrifices to reach his goal of making partner. He had worked hard and his legal reputation was growing. Hamilton, Hamilton and Clark paid him more money than he could ever have imagined earning.

Griffin read over a set of interrogatories, pausing to make notes here and there on a legal pad.

He leaned back in his chair, his eyes traveling to an elegantly framed photograph hanging on his wall. All of the associates had one in their office—it was a photo of the attorneys in the firm. Griffin's gaze landed on Marissa.

He had been fighting his feelings for Marissa for years. Griffin noticed her the very first day he walked through the doors of Hamilton, Hamilton and Clark. At the time, Marissa was in college—*too* young. She was also Jacob Hamilton Jr.'s daughter, which made her completely off-limits.

Now Marissa was all grown up. However, Griffin wanted to ensure that his career was firmly established before he settled down, which meant that falling in love with her would be a distraction he could not afford.

Marissa stepped out of the elevator and saw that Griffin was walking a client to the door. He stepped aside to let her enter through the mahogany doors.

She gave him a tiny smile of gratitude but did not linger.

A few minutes later, Griffin appeared in the doorway of her office. "You all right?" he asked. His gaze was as soft as a caress.

"I'm fine," Marissa responded with a nod.

Griffin's expression showed that he did not believe her. He walked all the way into her office and said, "Marissa, what's really going on? You look troubled about something."

She looked up, meeting his gaze. "It has nothing to do with work, Griff."

"Okay," he said, quickly backing off. "But if you need to talk…about any of your cases, you know where to find me."

She forced a smile. "I know. Thanks."

He was still watching her. Marissa thought she detected a flicker in his intense eyes, sending her pulse racing alarmingly.

Marissa noted how well the black suit fit his six-foot frame. She was entranced by his compelling personage. She found him very attractive. Griffin wore his hair cropped close and his dark brown eyes complemented his warm brown complexion. At thirty years old, Griffin tended to treat her as if she were years younger, when in fact there was only a four-year age difference between them.

She checked her watch. "I have about five minutes to prepare for a meeting," Marissa announced.

Taking the hint, Griffin nodded and headed to the door. "Don't forget what I said."

"I won't," Marissa responded as he walked out. Something in Griffin's manner always soothed her, which was why she'd often confided in him in the past. However, things had changed between them in the past few months, to the point that Marissa was somewhat surprised when Griffin had ventured into her office just now. Lately, the only time he stopped by was to discuss a case.

She released a soft sigh. Marissa had wanted to confide in Griffin, but the risk was much too high. She did not want what Harper had told her leaking out. She intended to have a conversation with Azure, as well. Clearly someone was out to hurt her family.

She was not about to let that happen.

After her meeting, Marissa worked in her office until three o'clock. It was a struggle for her to concentrate and she felt queasy, so she decided to go home. She packed up her briefcase, intending to get some work done there—locked in her bedroom. She just wanted to be alone.

Ten minutes later, she was in her BMW X5 and pulling out of the parking structure.

A wave of disappointment flowed through Marissa. After what Harper told her, she felt that everything she'd ever known about her parents had been a lie.

She had never heard her parents argue—they had always been very loving toward each other. So what would make her mother cheat on a man she proclaimed to love more than life itself?

As she neared home, Marissa released a soft sigh. She could hardly wait to get to her room and soak in a hot bath.

The Hamiltons had lived in the West Mt. Airy section of Philadelphia since the founding of the law firm. The neighborhood had a rich Revolutionary War history and featured a mosaic of restaurants, shops and cultural venues.

Marissa's eyes watered at the sight of Integrity, the

family homestead. She loved the late-1800s Victorian-style home that had been a staple in her family for two generations. All of her friends used to tease Marissa about living in a castle that came complete with turret and gargoyles. Her family later added a swimming pool and basketball and tennis courts.

She walked into the house, struggling to keep her expression blank. Marissa was hoping to avoid her mother and escape to her room. She was not ready to face Jeanette yet. She was still in shock from the news that Harper had given her.

"Marissa, dear," her mother greeted from the kitchen. She met Marissa at the bottom of the back stairs carrying a bottle of water. "How was your day at the office?"

"It was fine," she muttered in response.

"Your father and I are having dinner at Devon's tonight," Jeanette announced. "Why don't you join us? Your sister's going to meet us there."

Devon Seafood Grill was a favorite of hers, but Marissa really could not stomach being around her mother right now. "I'll just make something here," she told Jeanette. "I brought some work home with me."

"Dear, are you feeling well?" her mother inquired as she scanned Marissa's face. "You look a little peaked."

"I'm fine," Marissa lied. "I need to get started on this work."

She walked briskly out of the kitchen before Jeanette could utter a response.

Marissa rushed up the stairs and to her bedroom. She dropped her briefcase and purse on the bed before taking off for her bathroom.

When she walked out a few minutes later, she felt weak, but the queasiness was gradually dissipating.

She changed into a pair of sweats and an oversized T-shirt, then climbed into her bed and opened her briefcase.

There was a soft knock on her door before her mother popped her head inside.

"I didn't mean to disturb you, but I thought you could use some hot tea," Jeanette said as she walked into Marissa's bedroom. "I can tell that you are not feeling well."

Marissa accepted the tea with a grateful smile. "Thank you."

"Have you considered going to see Dr. Wallace?"

"Mother, I'm just tired," Marissa responded with a small sigh. "I don't need to see a doctor."

"Are you getting enough rest?" Jeanette asked. "I know how you lawyers tend to burn the candle at both ends."

Marissa was touched by her mother's concern, but she was also angry with her. She cleared her throat awkwardly before saying, "That's probably it, but I'll be fine. I'm going to take a hot bath and turn in pretty early tonight."

Jeanette studied her for a moment. "Marissa—"

"Mother, I really need to get some work done," she interjected. "The sooner I get it done, the sooner I can have that bath and get some rest."

"Okay, dear. I'll get out of here." Her mother backed off and headed to the door. "I'll see you in the morning."

Marissa shook her head sadly. She would never be able to look at her mother in the same way. Their relationship would never be the same.

Chapter 2

Thoughts of Marissa had consumed Griffin much of the evening and again this morning as he drove to work. He could not explain why he felt such a connection to this woman whose life experience was so different from his. The *why* really didn't matter, since Griffin did not intend to pursue her.

When Marissa had started working at the firm, she and Griffin had spent a lot of time together when Jacob assigned him to be a mentor to her. He was one of the few nonrelatives working at the firm and Jacob had thought Griffin would be a good fit for his daughter.

Griffin immediately recognized the desire and dedication in Marissa to become a successful attorney. While she lacked the confidence of her older sister, Jillian—who had quickly made a name for herself with a high-profile case involving a lawsuit between a rapper she'd gone to school with and his record label—Marissa had what it took to make it. She was only with the firm one year and she still had a lot to learn. He knew exactly how she felt; he'd been in that position himself years ago when Albert Clark had hired him.

Albert often told Griffin how much he reminded him of Albert at that age—an intelligent, motivated student with a passion for the law and no connections. He often advised Griffin to focus on his career for the time being.

Griffin took his advice. He grew up in the inner city and was the first person in his family to attend a four-year university, let alone obtain his law degree. Many of his classmates had gone to law school because they really did not have a clue as to what they wanted to do in life, but for Griffin, studying law was his dream.

For the Hamiltons, law seemed to be a family tradition. Griffin respected them all because they were good attorneys and they all seemed to have a passion for the law. He shared that same passion and drive. Griffin worked as hard as anyone else in the firm, if not harder at times. He wanted to prove himself and hoped to make partner one day.

To do that, he knew he'd have to make sacrifices, but he was constantly struggling where Marissa was concerned. She dominated his thoughts, causing him to fight his feelings on a daily basis. He would not risk the wrath of Jacob Hamilton, although Marissa was certainly worth it.

He really cared for Marissa, but constantly reminded himself that he could not let his emotions get in the way.

Too late.

Marissa stood in front of her full-length mirror eyeing her reflection. The antique mirror had once belonged to her paternal grandmother. The reflective glass offered a glimpse of how much Marissa resembled her father's mother.

She's Uncle Frank's mother, as well.

Marissa shook the thought of her uncle's affair with her mother out of her mind. She turned to get a side-view look at her appearance. Marissa's mouth tightened for a brief second. She removed the dress she had just slipped into moments before and tossed it carelessly across the room. It landed on her king-sized bed, joining a small pile of other abandoned clothing.

Marissa walked barefoot, crossing the room quickly. She entered her walk-in closet with purpose. She regretted not taking time the night before to find something to wear, and she did not want to be late for work. She had a meeting at nine o'clock with a client.

She chose a navy dress with a white Peter Pan collar and an empire waist. Marissa slipped into a pair of navy-and-white high-heeled pumps to match. She walked over to the mirror to check her reflection once more. Marissa brushed back her long brown hair and pulled it into a ponytail, securing it with a navy barrette. She scrutinized her appearance once more.

Although she was twenty-six years old, everyone seemed to think that she looked years younger. Maybe in time, Marissa would come to appreciate being considered so youthful looking, but for now she absolutely hated it.

As the youngest of Jacob and Jeanette's five children, she was babied by everyone. Growing up, she had always received special treatment, but lately, she had begun to feel that no one really took her seriously. Especially...

Marissa shook her head. No, she did not want to think about *him*.

"I am not going to let you ruin my day," she whispered.

Marissa glanced at the clock on her bedside table and then grabbed her purse. She needed to leave now if she planned to make it to the firm on time.

Her parents were seated at the table when she entered the kitchen.

"Good morning," Marissa said to no one in particular as she rushed in, grabbed a bottle of water, blew kisses toward them both and rushed out of the house.

Her father followed her. "Hey, that's all we get?"

Marissa smiled as she opened her car door. "Sorry about that, Daddy. I had a late start this morning and I have a meeting at nine. Are we still on for lunch?"

Jacob nodded.

"See you then," she responded, fighting back tears. "I need to leave."

He pressed a keypad on the wall to open the garage door.

Marissa waved and then backed her car out.

She loved her father dearly and it was killing her inside to carry this secret. Marissa could not understand how her mother could be so deceitful. How could she risk tearing her family apart by having an affair with Uncle Frank? He was her father's brother!

Poor Aunt Vanessa, she thought silently.

By the time Marissa arrived at the office, she was focused on business. She had always wanted to follow her siblings into law and worked very hard to make that happen, which included graduating from law school with honors.

Marissa was intent on showing her brothers and Jillian that she was every bit as good as they were, since they still seemed to treat her like the little baby sister who needed to be sheltered, despite the fact that there was only a five-year difference between her and Jake, her oldest brother.

Marissa wanted to be taken seriously by everyone, including her family. First, as an attorney, and then as a woman.

"Marissa, are you busy?"

She glanced up from her computer monitor to see Harper's new wife. "Azure, come in."

Azure closed the door behind her. "Harper told me about his conversation with you," she announced as she sat down in one of the visitor chairs.

"Someone contacted you anonymously claiming that my mother and my uncle had an affair."

Azure nodded.

"And that person also said that I am a result of that affair." It was more of a statement than a question. "Is there any proof of this, other than Uncle Frank confessing the truth to Harper?" Marissa wanted to know. "Do they have pictures of them leaving a hotel or something more scandalous?"

"Not that I know of," Azure responded. "Right now we have no other information, but in situations like this—all that is needed is a rumor, whether true or false."

Marissa settled back in her chair and crossed her legs. "So, what does this person want for this little tidbit? Money?"

"There's been no demand for money or anything. Marissa, I haven't taken this to my editor. You have to know that I am going to do everything I can to see that this accusation never sees the light of day."

"If your magazine doesn't publish the story, then I'm sure this person will go somewhere else. I really would like to know what's in it for them to try and ruin our lives." Marissa shook her head sadly.

"I can't imagine how you must be feeling right now," Azure told her. "I'm so sorry, Marissa."

"I still find it hard to believe that my…my mother could do something like this to my dad. They always seemed so happy and in love."

"I won't let this get out, Marissa."

"It may be out of your hands, Azure. Unfortunately, we will all have to wait and see if the other shoe falls."

Chapter 3

"Marissa, I can't thank you enough for everything you've done for me," a young woman said as they walked out of the courtroom.

Smiling, she responded, "You're welcome, Rita."

The twenty-year-old had pleaded no contest in a drunken-driving case. Marissa had suggested Rita plead to the charge of driving while visibly impaired.

"I've learned my lesson and I'll be relieved to be able to put this behind me."

"Will this charge be on my daughter's record forever?" the older woman with them asked. "I want her to have a chance to get a good job or become that doctor."

"If Rita stays out of trouble while she is on probation, then her record will be expunged. She will be able to do whatever she wants with her life." Marissa glanced over at the young girl. "It's all up to you, Rita."

"Lord knows, I pray so."

When her clients left, Marissa noticed a man standing near the exit doors of the courthouse. A smile tugged at her lips.

"Daddy, what are you doing here?" Marissa was surprised to see him. She had not noticed him in the courtroom, but then, she had been focused on helping her client.

"I came to watch my baby girl in action," he responded.

His words brought tears to her eyes. No other man would ever replace Jacob Hamilton Jr. as her father.

"You handled yourself well in there."

"It was an easy case," Marissa responded.

"And you did a good job," her father insisted as he wrapped an arm around her. "Just remember this feeling on those days when the case is a difficult one."

"Thanks, Daddy."

They walked out to their cars.

"Why don't I call your mother and have her meet us for lunch?" Jacob suggested.

"I have a better idea," Marissa countered. "Why don't you and Mother have lunch together? I need to get back to the office." She could not stomach being around her mother right now.

He scanned her face as if he was trying to read her expression. "Is there something going on between you and your mom?"

Jacob's question surprised Marissa. "No, things are fine. I've just been really busy, Daddy."

"You're too busy to grab a bite to eat?"

"I'll get something on the way back to the office."

"Okay," Jacob said. "I'll see you later, baby girl."

She walked away briskly and headed to the nearest exit door.

Within minutes, Marissa was inside her car and on the way back to the office. She was in a great mood after her victory in court—it was a small one, but a victory nonetheless.

Jillian and her brothers were all waiting for Marissa when she arrived.

"So, how did it go?" Jake asked. "Did she plead no contest?"

Marissa nodded. "Rita was given probation. I believe she has learned her lesson from this experience."

"Her mother is really sweet," Jake stated. He and Rita's older brother had gone to college together and were in the same fraternity.

"Please tell me that you all are not going to be sitting here in my office like this every time I go to court."

Jillian laughed. "You might as well get used to the idea, Marissa. They treated me the same way when I started."

"Me, too," Marcus interjected. "And I bet Dad was at the courthouse, wasn't he?"

"Yes, he was there," Marissa confirmed. "Every case so far."

"He still comes to see me in action," Jillian stated.

"He comes to mine, too," Anthony interjected.

Marissa looked over at Jake. "When did Dad stop coming to yours?"

Jake laughed. "When you started working here."

Smiling, Marissa shooed everyone out of her office. "I need to get back to work and I'm sure you all need to do the same. *Leave.*"

Her first year at the law firm had been a success, as far as Marissa was concerned. She never thought she could work any harder than she did in law school, but Hamilton, Hamilton and Clark was a real pressure cooker at times.

There had been days when Marissa thought she would crack under the strain of it all, but she would never share this with any of her family members. It would just confirm for them that she was not able to handle the pressures of being an attorney.

The only person with whom she could be completely honest about her feelings was Griffin. He understood how she felt and never once judged her. She recalled a conversation they had had when she first started working at the firm. They were in his office going over a case.

"Griffin, can I ask you something?" Marissa had asked him.

"Sure."

"Do you think I have it easier than the other associates because I am a Hamilton? I want you to be honest with me."

He met her gaze and responded, "I believe you didn't have to work hard to become an associate here after graduating from law school, but I know that your father treats all of his associates equally. It's one of the things I respect most about him."

"I wish everyone was as open-minded and observant as you."

"Don't let office rumors get into your head," Griffin advised. *"You can't stop others from talking, but you*

do not have to give their words power. Stay focused on
what's important, and that's proving yourself."

"Eminence just did an article on my family, and
when you look at the photos, we look like a modern-day
version of the Cosby family—picture-perfect."

He grinned. "Are you saying that you're not?"

Marissa smiled. "You know the answer to that just
from the amount of time you've spent around Jake and
Harper. I love my brother and my cousin, but I hate
how competitive they are with each other."

"It keeps them both on their toes," Griffin stated. "I
wouldn't worry about them."

Marissa's attention returned to the present.

Her family was anything but picture-perfect. Un-
spoken tensions that lay rumbling beneath the surface
threatened to topple them all.

"How did it go in court today?" Griffin asked as he
held the elevator door open for Marissa.

"Great," she said. "Rita should get probation and if
she stays out of trouble, she'll be able to return to college and finish her degree."

He glanced at Marissa as the elevator doors closed
on the two of them, alone in the car. That's what made
her a good lawyer and a good person. How much she
cared for her clients. She was as beautiful on the inside
as she was on the outside.

She was also incredibly sexy, despite her conserva-
tive dress.

And she wasn't afraid of hard work.

These were just a few of the reasons why he loved her.

He pulled up short as he stole another glance her way. Loved her?

He felt a strange sensation in his gut as he finally admitted it. Yes, he loved the very woman who was off-limits.

Marissa was surprised when she glimpsed her aunt in the hallway a couple of days later. Vanessa Bonnard was a renowned fashion designer who traveled frequently. She rarely made visits to the firm whenever she was home. In fact, she rarely attended any family functions—unless there were media involved.

"Aunt Vanessa," she murmured in greeting. Marissa struggled to meet her aunt's intense gaze. Her mother and Vanessa had never been close, but her aunt had always treated Marissa kindly.

"Hello, Marissa. How are you?"

"I'm fine."

Vanessa's gaze left her face and traveled downward briefly. "What a beautiful dress," she said with a smile. "It's quite lovely on you."

"Thank you," Marissa responded. "I didn't know that you were back from Milan."

"I arrived last night. I thought I'd surprise my husband for an early lunch, but it seems that he'll be in court all day."

"They usually break for lunch around this time. Why don't you give him a call?" Marissa suggested.

Vanessa smiled. "I just may do that. Thanks, sweetie."

"You're welcome," Marissa said. "Well, I guess I had better get back to my desk. It's good seeing you, Aunt Vanessa."

"You know…why don't you join us, Marissa?" Vanessa blocked her path. "We hardly get to spend any time together. C'mon, it will be fun to catch up."

"Oh no," Marissa responded quickly. "You and Uncle Frank should spend some quality time together. You just got back."

She certainly could not handle having lunch with the man who could be her father. Marissa was not interested in any family reunions of this kind.

"Oh, but we would love for you to join us," Vanessa said smoothly.

"Maybe next time," Marissa told her.

Vanessa smiled. "I'm going to hold you to that."

Marissa gave her a slight nod. She was grateful when her assistant interrupted them regarding a trial date.

When they were alone, she turned her attention back to her aunt.

Vanessa chuckled. "You know…that expression on your face…you look just like Frank. My husband makes that face whenever he is silently contemplating something. I guess it must be hereditary."

"I really need to get back to my desk," Marissa blurted. "I have some phone calls to make."

"Enjoy the rest of your day, sweetie."

"You, too," she said. Marissa thought she glimpsed something in Vanessa's eyes, but it vanished as quickly as it had come. For a moment, it looked like displeasure, but she could not be sure.

Marissa walked briskly to her office. She was barely aware of Harper's presence. He must have followed her.

"Hey, what were you and my mom talking about?" Harper asked in a low voice. "I saw you two in the hall."

Marissa glanced over at him. "She invited me to lunch. I turned her down."

"How did she seem?"

"Same as always," Marissa said. "Why? Do you think she knows anything? Please tell me that you didn't tell her."

"I didn't say anything to my mother and I don't plan to. If anyone tells her, it should be my father."

"Nobody should say anything to anybody," Marissa declared. "Just let them both take it to the grave. My dad does not deserve to be hurt. Neither does Aunt Vanessa."

"Knowing my mother, she would find a way to make Dad pay if she ever found out," Harper said.

Chapter 4

"Are you feeling okay?"

Marissa looked up from the notes she and her assistant were going over in one of the conference rooms. She gave her a slight nod. "I think I'm coming down with a cold. I'll be fine, though."

"Why don't I make you a cup of tea? You can close your door and lie down on your couch for a while. You don't have any appointments until later today."

"Some tea would be nice, Roberta. Thank you," Marissa murmured. The idea of taking a nap was very appealing to her. She was feeling a bit tired.

She was in her office and sitting on the couch when Roberta entered the room carrying a cup of hot tea.

Marissa smiled as she accepted the tea from her assistant. "Thanks so much."

"Go on and rest. I'll see that no one disturbs you."

Marissa began to feel better almost as soon as she lay down.

She could hear Griffin outside her office talking to one of the other associates. Marissa loved the sound of his voice. He reminded her of the smooth, late-night disc jockeys on the radio.

Marissa allowed her memory to drift into forbidden territory—one night five months ago. She had decided to work late. She had been surprised to find that Griffin was also there after everyone had already gone home. They decided to take their laptops into a conference room to work while they shared a dinner of shrimp fried rice, orange chicken and egg drop soup.

Maybe it was the adrenaline of working on a case; maybe it was sleep deprivation or maybe it was just inevitable, but Marissa and Griffin could no longer ignore their mutual attraction.

They soon decided to call it a night.

Marissa followed Griffin to his apartment. As soon as they were inside, they were in each other's arms.

Griffin had undressed her slowly and then carried her into his bedroom.

He laid her on the bed. Griffin removed his own clothing before joining her.

"I've wanted this for a long time," he whispered.

"So have I," Marissa admitted.

Griffin captured her lips with his own, holding her close to his nakedness.

Marissa moaned softly as her passion ignited into a flame in the pit of her belly. She burned with desire for Griffin's touch.

They had made love slowly that night, not wanting the moment to come to an end.

Marissa could still feel the heat of their passion from that night—it burned in her memory. The sweetness of his kisses lingered in her mind, filling her with the desire to be kissed by Griffin again.

But that night was long gone.

The special moment they had shared was just that—a moment.

As soon as the thought revealed itself, Marissa shook her head in denial. What she had shared with Griffin that night was only meant to last for a moment, but for Marissa, it would last a lifetime.

Marissa closed her eyes and drifted off to sleep with Griffin consuming her thoughts.

When she woke up, Marissa could not believe that almost two hours had passed, but she felt so much better now and more energetic. She rose to her feet and went to the bathroom to wash her face.

"You look like you're feeling better," Roberta commented when Marissa came out.

"I do," she responded. "I feel so much better."

It was almost time for her meeting with a new client, so Marissa spent the next half hour going over the file her assistant had prepared.

"Hey, what are you doing? In here playing lawyer?"

Marissa looked up and grinned at her oldest brother. "What are *you* doing?"

Jake strolled casually into the room. "What's that supposed to mean?" he asked with a sly smile.

"You are no angel," she stated.

"How's it going?" he inquired with a grin. "I know

how overwhelming working here can be. Not to mention working with family."

"I'm hanging in there."

"Well, let me know if I can help you with anything."

"You really don't have to worry about me, Jake," Marissa said. "I'm fine. I can handle my job."

"I just want to make sure that you're not taking on more than you can handle."

Marissa did not bother to disguise her irritation. "I am not a baby, Jake. I don't need you looking over my shoulder. Why don't you focus your energies on your new wife?"

He ignored her remark. "It's just that your sister said that you've been pretty moody lately."

"Maybe all of you should just leave me alone," Marissa sniped at her brother. She took in a deep breath, releasing it slowly.

"I'm sorry, Jake. I should not be snapping at you like this. It's just that I've been with the firm a year now and I feel I'm doing a great job, but it's frustrating when you all keep looking over my shoulder. I can't breathe this way."

He nodded in understanding. "I'll back off, Marissa."

She smiled. "Thanks."

Marissa leaned back in her chair. She hoped that Jake would keep his word. Now if she could get the rest of her siblings to do the same.

One of the other qualities that Griffin loved about Marissa was her genuine smile, which seemed prominently on display at all times. She had a wonderful sense of humor and loved to laugh.

Griffin released a sigh. He missed her laughter.

He also missed spending time with her.

The memory of the one night they had shared flashed to the forefront of his mind. What he and Marissa shared that night had been beautiful. Griffin held on to that memory as if it were a lifeline. He never wanted to forget the way she looked at him as they made love or the way her lips felt against his.

A tremor of disappointment slid down his spine because he knew that they would never share another night like that one. The experience was once-in-a-lifetime. Still, he couldn't turn off his feelings for Marissa as if they were controlled by a switch. And those feelings frightened him.

It was time for a reality check.

He had crossed the line when he slept with Marissa.

Afterward, he had apologized for taking advantage of Marissa, although she tried to assure him that she did not feel that way.

Marissa confessed her attraction to him and assured Griffin that she wanted him to make love to her.

Griffin told her that it should not ever happen again. He and Marissa both had worked hard to prove themselves at the firm—if word ever got out that he had slept with the boss's daughter, he would be fired, and Marissa's reputation would never be the same. Griffin did not want to see her hurt beyond that one night, so he told her that they should keep a professional distance going forward.

Professional distance. It was one of the hardest things to do. He hungered for Marissa's touch, her kisses… Griffin could not stomach the thought of Marissa with another man. He did not even want to think about the idea, despite the fact that they had no future together.

Griffin shook his head, trying to erase the image of the beautiful woman who dominated his thoughts.

As if he conjured her, Marissa appeared in his doorway. "Didn't mean to disturb you," she said. "Daddy wanted me to tell you that he can meet with you right now if you have some time. He's thinking about coming in late tomorrow."

He silently took in her appearance. Marissa was as beautiful as ever, although there was something different about her—something he could not put a finger on. Griffin did not like the gulf that existed between them. They used to be able to talk easily, but now... well, things were different.

"Thanks, Marissa."

"Not a problem." She turned to leave.

"Hey," he called out. "Do you have a few minutes?"

"Sure."

"How are things going with you?" Griffin asked her. "I know we haven't had a real chance to sit down and talk about your development, but—"

"Everything is good," Marissa interjected a little too quickly.

He pointed to a chair. "Would you like to sit down?"

Marissa shook her head. "I really need to get going, Griff. Besides, my dad is waiting to meet with you."

There was more that Griffin wanted to say to Marissa, but he simply nodded. Things were different between them now for sure—and it was all his fault.

He reined in his errant thoughts and went back to

work, until his cell phone rang just as he was preparing to leave the office.

"Hello."

"Griffin, hey…it's me, Colin. I know this is late notice, but we're playing at the Blue Nile in Center City tonight. If you don't have any plans, why don't you come out? I would love to catch up."

"Sounds like a plan," Griffin responded. "I'm on my way home. Give me a chance to freshen up and I'll see you shortly."

Griffin normally did not go out on weeknights, but because he had not seen his friend in months, he made an exception. He and Colin were childhood friends who grew up in the same neighborhood. While he had chased after his dream of being a lawyer, Colin had chased after his music. He was a phenomenal keyboard player.

Griffin was actually looking forward to seeing Colin and his band perform. Years ago, he used to sing with them, but only to help earn money for college. He never seriously considered pursuing music as a career. His first love had always been law.

For a brief second Griffin considered calling Marissa and inviting her to join him, but he changed his mind. Things were still very awkward between them.

"I don't know why I let you talk me into this," Marissa told her friend.

"Because you need a night out," Cheryl responded with a smile. "I bet you haven't been to the Blue Nile in forever. Besides, we haven't spent much time together lately. I want to know what's going on with you."

Cheryl had been Marissa's best friend since high

school. She regretted not having enough time to see her regularly. "I've been working hard to stay on top of my caseload."

The place was crowded. Marissa glanced around, scanning the room for an empty table. They found one in a corner and sat down.

"How do you like teaching at Temple?" Marissa asked.

"I love it," her friend said. "What about you? Are you still loving law?"

Marissa nodded. "It's a lot of work, but I do enjoy it. What I don't like about the job is working with family. They treat me like a child—watching over me and constantly checking on me."

Cheryl laughed. "What did you expect? You are the youngest in the family. My little sister complains of the same thing."

"Obviously, not this. Your sister is only fourteen. I am a grown woman."

"The last time we talked, you were telling me about this guy you work with," Cheryl said with a grin. "How is that going?"

"We work together," Marissa responded. "That's about it."

"What happened?"

Marissa shrugged. "He has this thing about not getting involved with the boss's daughter. He loves his job and apparently it means more to him than I do."

"How does it make you feel?"

Marissa met her friend's gaze. "I wish my name was something other than Hamilton at times. This guy—he's great and I understand his feelings, but I just thought that… Anyway, it doesn't matter what I thought. We decided it was best to keep a professional relationship."

A waiter appeared to take their order.

Marissa ordered a glass of water.

"You're not drinking tonight?" Cheryl questioned. "Not even a glass of wine?"

"No, I have an early day tomorrow."

The band members took their places onstage.

"Have you heard them before?" Marissa asked her friend.

Cheryl nodded. "A couple of times. They're really good."

Marissa settled back to listen to the band. Truthfully she was grateful to be away from the house. Her mother should be asleep by the time Marissa arrived home later in the evening. She was still trying to avoid her mother as much as possible.

She bobbed her head to the music. "This band is great."

Cheryl agreed.

Marissa's eyes traveled the crowded room. There were a lot of people out tonight. The first time she had ever come to the Blue Nile Club was with Griffin. They had come here to celebrate the win of her first case.

She enjoyed being here with Cheryl, but it reminded Marissa of Griffin. Even now, she felt his presence.

Marissa gave herself a mental shake. There was no use thinking about a man who would never return her feelings.

Chapter 5

Seated in front of the stage, Griffin tapped his foot to the music. It had been a while since he'd been out like this, relaxing and listening to a live band. He made a mental note to change that going forward. It was fine to stay focused on work, but Griffin realized that he also needed some downtime to relax. It wasn't healthy to hold on to pent-up emotions and energies.

The room exploded in applause when the song ended.

Onstage, Colin took the microphone. "It's wonderful to be back home in Philly," he said.

"Welcome home," someone in the audience yelled out.

He laughed. "I have a special treat for you tonight. Who remembers the tall, cool dude that used to sing with us?"

Several people in the audience clapped and screamed in memory.

Colin laughed. "Well, we have Griff in the audience and—"

The sound of applause drowned out the rest of Colin's words.

Smiling, Griffin met his friend's gaze and shook his head. He had not come here to perform. It had been years since he had been on a stage. He had planned to just come out, listen to music and reconnect with old friends.

Colin refused to take no for an answer. "You hear that applause—that's for you, bro," he told Griffin. "C'mon…"

Griffin rose to his feet and made his way up to the stage.

Colin handed him the mike.

Music filled the stage and its surroundings.

Griffin moved to its beat and began to sing. He soon felt as if he had never left the stage and he allowed his love for music to take over.

Marissa could not believe her eyes when Griffin walked up on the stage. She had no idea he could sing.

"I don't believe it," Marissa uttered.

"What is it?" Cheryl asked. "You know him?"

She nodded. "That's Griff."

"The guy you work with? The one you've been telling me about?"

"Yes," Marissa responded.

Marissa was very entranced by the bass timbre of his voice. Griffin had never shared this side of himself with her before. Obviously, they were not as close as she had imagined.

As if drawn by an invisible web, Griffin met her gaze.

His eyes registered surprise, but he never interrupted his singing.

"He has a nice voice," Cheryl said.

Marissa agreed.

Griffin received a standing ovation and thunderous applause as he thanked everyone and left the stage. Instead of returning to his table, he walked over to where she and Cheryl were sitting.

Marissa spoke first, making the introductions before saying, "I didn't know about this side of you."

He met her gaze and then smiled. "This is the first time I've been on a stage in forever. When I left the band, I never really thought much about it. It just became a part of my past once I passed the bar."

"You never really talk about your life."

Griffin shrugged in nonchalance. "There isn't a lot to tell."

"Well, I guess I didn't know you as well as I thought I did." Marissa tried to hide the disappointment she felt. She had shared so much of herself with Griffin, even her personal feelings and insecurities.

Apparently there was much to Griffin that he'd kept private.

"I enjoyed your singing," Cheryl told him.

"So did I," Marissa interjected after a moment. "You can really sing."

"Thank you both," Griffin replied with a smile. "I didn't know that you liked places like this, Marissa. I figured you were more of a jazz lover."

Cheryl chuckled. "Marissa…she hates jazz."

"No, I don't," she countered. "I just like classic R & B more."

She was saved from further embarrassment when the band took a break and Griffin introduced them to Cheryl and Marissa.

Marissa was thrilled that she had decided to come out with Cheryl. She was really having a great time. It was nice to see Griffin relaxed and having a good time. She really liked this side of him and wished he would display it more.

Marissa was in love with Griffin Jackson and there was a time when she had hoped he felt the same way. But it soon became obvious that he did not return her feelings.

So what else could she do?

After their one night together, Griffin told her that their making love had been impulsive and ill-advised. He decided that they should keep their relationship professional.

Wounded, Marissa had simply agreed. She told Griffin that no one would ever know what had happened that night, and that it would never happen again.

However, it did not stop her heart from aching for him. But Marissa was not going to force herself on Griffin. She tried to keep her distance as much as she could when they were in the office. They were exceedingly polite with each other, careful not to exchange more than casual pleasantries.

In the beginning, Marissa tried to convince herself that this was all for the best. That was before she saw the plus line in the home pregnancy test.

* * *

It had never once occurred to Marissa that she was pregnant. She and Griffin had used a condom the night they made love, so she had no real reason to suspect anything. She had ignored the symptoms for weeks, chalking up the missed period and the constant nausea to stress.

By the time Marissa decided to take a pregnancy test, she was about nine weeks along. Stunned beyond words, she had no idea what to do. A baby was the last thing she needed right now, and she was sure Griffin would feel the same way.

She knew that many early pregnancies ended in miscarriage, so Marissa decided to keep mum. There was no point in alarming her family or Griffin unnecessarily.

For a brief moment, she had even considered terminating the pregnancy, but once she heard the baby's heartbeat, everything changed for Marissa.

You are my baby. I am going to do everything in my power to protect you.

There were two questions that stayed at the forefront of her mind these days. How was she going to tell Griffin?

Should she tell him?

Marissa's eyes traveled downward. Eventually she was not going to be able to hide her pregnancy anymore. She was already struggling to wear clothes that would camouflage the roundness of her belly. Marissa had also taken to carrying large handbags—something she used to avoid because of her five-foot-two-inch frame. She still favored high-heeled shoes, but she had to consider lowering them some during her pregnancy.

Her mind traveled back to Griffin.

Marissa was dreading his reaction, and silently rationalized that she had not told him because she could never find the *right* time.

She couldn't just blurt it out, but Marissa vowed to tell Griffin as soon as the time was right.

Chapter 6

The next day, Griffin was back to his usual self in the office. The only time he had stopped by Marissa's office was to ask her to keep quiet about his singing.

"Why do you want to keep something like this a secret? You have a beautiful voice, Griff."

"I don't want anyone thinking or assuming that my loyalties are divided. Your father and Albert frown on associates taking on anything that might take the focus off being a good lawyer."

"I understand," Marissa said. She knew that he was correct. The partners of the firm demanded complete loyalty from all of the associates, including her. "I won't say a word."

Griffin thanked her and was gone without another word.

Marissa turned her attention back to her computer monitor.

It was not easy working in the same office as Griffin. Her feelings for him made it a daily challenge. Then there was the fact that she was carrying his baby.

She couldn't keep her mind off the baby for the rest of the day. She was still thinking about it when she walked into Integrity shortly after six o'clock that evening.

"Marissa, I'm glad you're here," her mother said as soon as she opened the door.

She glanced up at her sister and then her mother. "Why, what's going on?"

"I thought we'd have dinner out," Jeanette announced cheerfully. "Just us girls."

"You two go ahead," Marissa suggested. "I'm going to have a hot bath and then watch some TV. I'm in the mood to do absolutely nothing."

Her mother seemed disappointed. "Honey, you have to eat. We haven't spent any time together in weeks."

"I'll eat something if I get hungry," Marissa told her. "You and Jillian have fun."

"You're sure you don't want to join us? We hardly see you these days and we all live in the same house."

"We'll do it another time," Marissa promised.

She was very angry with her mother. At some point, they would have to sit down and have a discussion, but Marissa was not ready for that. Some of the shock had worn off, but it was still too soon.

"Marissa, have you been sleeping?" her doctor asked.

"More than usual," she responded. "I've been trying to clear my caseload so that when the baby comes…"

He nodded in understanding. "You look tired. Are you taking your vitamins?"

"I am," Marissa said. "Dr. Benton, I haven't been able to really keep any food down. I thought the morning sickness would be gone by now."

"It should ease up and you'll begin to feel a whole lot better."

She had read up on what to expect in her pregnancy. She knew her baby was about the size of an avocado, that the eyes were closer to the front of the head and the ears in close to their final position. Marissa felt a surge of excitement every time she heard her baby's heartbeat, and she yearned to be able to share this with someone. Even her best friend had no idea that she was pregnant.

Marissa held her secret close to her because she did not want to admit that she had made a huge mistake by having sex with Griffin. In fact, she had no right to judge her mother so harshly, but Jeanette was a married woman, whereas she and Griffin were both single.

She left the doctor's office and drove straight to work. Marissa would have to say something soon because she'd be showing shortly. Meantime, she did not want any rumors spoiling her secret before she had a chance to prepare her family.

At the office she saw Griffin, Jake and Harper in a conference room discussing some case. From the looks of it, her brother and cousin were on opposite ends. Nothing new there.

Poor Griff, she thought. He was caught in the middle and trying to play peacemaker.

Marissa hoped that her baby shared Griffin's handsome features, especially his long lashes and perfectly shaped lips.

He glanced up and saw her in the hallway.

Embarrassed at being caught staring at him, Marissa gave a tiny wave and headed to her office.

The next morning, all of the associates gathered for the weekly staff meeting.

Marissa grabbed a bottle of water and sat down beside her brother Marcus. She had some saltines in the pocket of her jacket, in case she needed to eat something to settle her stomach. Marissa hoped to make it through the meeting without experiencing a bout of nausea. She did not want her family or Griffin becoming suspicious.

Griffin walked in a few minutes later and sat down at the conference table in the empty chair across from her.

"Victor Ewing was arrested last night at the airport," Jacob announced. "The federal authorities spent three years looking for this guy. He's wanted on tax-evasion charges."

"He wants us to represent him?" Jake inquired. "What happened with his last attorney?"

"Is he the guy who left the country before they could arrest him?" Jillian asked. "He owned several hair salons."

"I remember reading something about this," Marissa interjected. "He went to Nigeria and the authorities were not able to extradite him. Why did he come back to the U.S.?"

"His mother is gravely ill and Victor mistakenly believed that the statute of limitations had expired. It is one of the reasons he fired his last attorney. Victor believes that the feds were tipped off. He says that the only person who knew he had come back was his attorney."

"I'd like to meet with Mr. Ewing," Marcus stated. "This is the type of challenging case I've been looking for."

"Do we even want to represent a man like Victor Ewing?" Jillian asked. "The cost to try a case like this is going to cost at least a million dollars. Does he even have any money?"

"He's facing four counts of filing false tax returns and two counts of structuring financial transactions to avoid reporting requirements," Jacob said. "The feds say that he also used business proceeds to buy a million-dollar home in New Jersey, and to transfer funds to Nigeria."

Marissa could feel the heat of Griffin's gaze as he silently observed her. She kept her expression blank. She was afraid that he might see the truth that she was keeping something from him.

After the meeting, Harper followed Marissa into her office.

"How are you doing?" he asked.

"As well as can be expected," she said. "How about you?"

"Same here."

Marissa gave him a sidelong glance. "How are things going between you and Uncle Frank?"

"I don't have a whole lot to say to him," Harper said. "We don't talk unless we have to, and that's mostly here in the office. By the way, your mom invited all of us over for one of the Hamilton family dinners on Sunday."

Marissa groaned. "I don't want to do this."

Harper nodded in agreement. "Neither do I. In fact, Azure and I won't be in attendance."

"You should rethink your decision," Marissa said. "I think we should both attend—if we don't, then the rest of the family may get suspicious. That's the last thing we need."

Chapter 7

Marissa was relieved when Jake and his wife, Charlotte, arrived on Sunday. Jeanette could then take her focus off Marissa. Her mother had been trying to engage her in conversation all morning. Marissa just wanted to get through this family dinner so that she could retreat to her bedroom. She was not feeling well and had experienced momentary bouts of nausea.

While Jeanette was engaged in a conversation with Charlotte, Marissa hid out in the kitchen. She checked on the food before setting the table in the massive dining room.

Marcus arrived next.

He glanced at his sister, saying, "Marissa, are you putting on weight?"

"That's a question no girl likes to hear," Marissa responded as casually as she could manage.

"It looks good on you," Marcus assured her. "In fact,

you're glowing. I guess we're not working you too hard from the looks of it."

She smiled. "Trust me, I work hard enough."

When Harper and Azure walked into the house, Marissa met them in the living room. "I'm so glad you both came."

"My mom and dad won't be here," Harper announced. "I can't say that I'm disappointed, though."

Marissa agreed.

The rest of her siblings arrived, as did Harper's.

They all gathered in the spacious family room, talking until Jeanette announced dinner was served.

The evening turned out to be a pleasant one, and despite everything that was going on, Marissa managed to enjoy herself.

She was exhausted by the time everyone left.

"Where are you going?" her father asked when she was going upstairs. "You're not abandoning us, are you?"

"I'm going to my room to do some reading before I go to bed."

"Why don't you watch a movie with us? Your mother and I were just about to start it."

"Daddy, I just want to sit down and really enjoy my book. I don't remember the last time I read a novel for fun."

"Marissa, I know that there is something going on between you and your mother. She is just as confused as I am. Now, why don't you tell me why you are being so distant?"

She released a soft sigh. "Daddy, there's nothing wrong."

"Are you sure?" he asked.

Jacob gazed at her, studying her expression. "Okay," he said after a moment.

Jeanette walked into the hallway carrying a bowl of hot, buttery popcorn. "Ready?" she asked.

He nodded and then went into the family room.

Her mother looked at her. "Are you joining us?"

Marissa shook her head. "I'm going upstairs to do some reading. I'll see you all in the morning."

Then she rushed off to her room before her parents tried to get her to stay and watch the movie with them—something she often did. But now things were different.

Marissa walked into the employee break room. She spotted one of the paralegals named Sue and sat down at the table beside her. Sue was pregnant and Marissa enjoyed talking to her about her baby. It was easy to see the woman was thrilled.

"When is your baby due?" she asked Sue.

"In January," she responded with a smile.

Marissa did not mention that she was also pregnant. "You look beautiful. Pregnancy agrees with you."

"You're so sweet. I have to admit that I have really enjoyed being pregnant. I didn't have morning sickness like most women."

"Lucky you," Marissa murmured. Too bad she couldn't say the same thing.

Sue rubbed her swollen belly. "I'm having a boy."

Marissa grinned. "Congratulations. That's wonderful."

"We're very excited," Sue said. "My husband and I both wanted a boy."

Marissa wondered what she was carrying. Would her baby be a boy who looked just like Griffin? For a moment she wondered what Griffin would prefer—a boy he could teach to play sports…or a daughter he could pamper?

When she left the break room a few minutes later, Marissa ran into Griffin, who had just returned to the office. She had heard that he had been in court most of the morning.

"Hey, I've been meaning to ask you something," Griffin began. "Are you upset with me?"

Marissa shook her head no. "Why should I be upset with you?"

"That night—"

She cut him off by saying, "This has nothing to do with you. I'm just in a bad mood right now, Griff. It's probably best to just leave me alone and let me deal with this."

"Deal with what?" he asked, looking puzzled.

Marissa waved her hands. "It's nothing really."

"This isn't like you at all, Marissa."

"This is me tired, overworked and buried under a pile of cases I need to review. Law school was a piece of cake compared to this."

Griffin smiled. "I've had days like that, but it does get better."

"I know," Marissa murmured. "I love being a lawyer. I'm just feeling a bit overwhelmed right now." She didn't add that being nauseated and carrying around a family secret did not help.

"Sure there's nothing I can do to help?" Griffin inquired.

Marissa shook her head. "You have quite a load on your plate, as well. Besides, I need to work this all out myself. I don't want anyone here thinking that being a Hamilton gives me a free ride."

"I know how hard you work around here," he told her. "No one in their right mind will think something like that when it comes to you, Marissa."

She gave him a wry smile. "You'd be surprised."

Griffin decided to grab a bite to eat before going home.

He walked across the street to a restaurant and spotted Marissa seated in a booth alone. She was reading the menu and apparently had not seen him.

Griffin approached her. "Mind if I join you?"

She was clearly surprised to see him. "I don't know, Griff. Is this considered keeping a professional distance?"

He was taken off guard by her response. "I never meant that we couldn't be friends, Marissa. I am still your mentor and I would like to also be your friend."

"I don't think you know what you want, Griff."

"Earlier today, I asked if you were angry with me," he said. "I'm sorry, Marissa. I never meant to hurt you."

She met his gaze. "Not everything going on in my life is about you."

Griffin sat down across from her.

"How is the Ponzi-scheme case going?" she asked, picking up her menu.

He signaled for the server to bring him one. "It's going okay. There are many angry people out there."

"They lost money," Marissa stated.

She cleared her throat softly. "Tell me something, Griff. How do you feel about defending a case like this?"

"To be honest, I am not convinced that we are representing a guilty man. I think Blaine Morton is just another victim—a scapegoat for something bigger."

"Do you think you will be able to prove it?" Marissa asked.

He smiled. "It's not our job to prove innocence, just cast doubt in the minds of jurors that the defendant is guilty."

"That doesn't exactly make us sound like heroes," she murmured.

The server returned to the table ready to take their order.

When Griffin was undecided, Marissa surveyed him for a moment and then said, "You look like a Cajun chicken pasta kind of man."

He laughed and nodded. "I'll have that."

Griffin met Marissa's gaze. "And I believe the lady will have the fire-grilled salmon."

She smiled and nodded.

His cell phone rang.

"Are you going to take that?" Marissa asked. "It could be important."

"They can leave a message. I'm enjoying dinner with a colleague and friend."

She did not respond, leaving Griffin to wonder if he had said something to upset her.

Chapter 8

Bored, Marissa surfed through the channels on television in the family room, searching for something interesting to watch.

Her mother walked into the room. "How are you feeling, sugar?" She sat down on the chair across from Marissa.

Marissa could feel her mother's eyes on her and shifted uncomfortably in her seat. She picked up a pillow and placed it in front of her stomach. "I'm okay. I think it was something I ate that just didn't agree with me." The housekeeper had informed her mother earlier that Marissa was in her bathroom throwing up.

"Are you hungry? You haven't eaten anything today."

Marissa shook her head. She did not believe she could keep anything down. She was looking forward to this nausea phase of her pregnancy ending.

"I think you're working much too hard, Marissa."

Jeanette's words broke through her musings. "You're sure you don't want to try eating something?"

Marissa shook her head. "Not right now, Mother. Maybe in a little while." She felt so disappointed in her mother, which made it difficult to hold a pleasant conversation with her.

"Did I do something to upset you?" Jeanette blurted. "We've always been so close, Marissa. Why can't you talk to me?"

"There isn't anything to talk about," she responded.

"I don't know why you feel that I'm upset with you. Are you feeling guilty about something?"

Jeanette opened her mouth and then closed it. After a moment, she uttered, "I think I'll go make a few phone calls."

Marissa knew that she had hurt her mother's feelings, but that pain could never compare to the one Jeanette had inflicted on her.

"Where's Mom and Dad?" Jillian asked when she entered the kitchen. She had just arrived home from the office.

"I left Daddy at the office," Marissa announced. "I haven't seen Mom. She wasn't home when I got here."

"Daddy left shortly after you did," Jillian commented. "I'm surprised Mom is not here. She's usually home by now," Jillian said. "It's nine o'clock. Mom doesn't like to be out alone at night."

Maybe she was not alone, Marissa thought silently. The thought had not occurred to her before, but maybe her mother was using the planning of the charity gala as a means to have an affair. Jeanette was the chairperson of the planning committee for the Hearts and Hands Charity Ball, which benefited the Tuck Me In Foundation. The annual fundraiser was very close to her heart.

"What are you thinking about?" Jillian asked, cutting into her thoughts. "Marissa, you've been in a strange mood for weeks now. What's going on with you?"

"I don't know what you're talking about," Marissa said.

Jillian openly studied her sister's face. "You're my sister and I know you well. Something is going on with you—I'm sure of it."

"I just have a lot on my plate right now. I need to stay focused."

"Do you need help with anything?"

Marissa stiffened. "No, it's not that at all. Look, Jillian, I may be the youngest in the family, but I'm more than capable of pulling my own weight."

"Sorry," Jillian uttered. "Didn't mean to offend you."

"I shouldn't have snapped at you," Marissa confessed. "I know you were only trying to help." She had never been a moody person, but lately, her moods seemed to shift constantly.

"Marissa, if you need to talk about anything, I'm here for you."

"I know that."

They looked up when they heard the front door open and close. Jeanette walked in. "Mom, where have you been?" Marissa asked. "You are not usually out so late by yourself."

"I had dinner with a couple of friends," Jeanette said. She glanced over at Marissa. "What's wrong, dear?"

"Nothing," she said. "I was just wondering where

you could be. I know that planning meetings do not last this long."

Jeanette gave a short chuckle. "Do I have a curfew now?"

"No, but you should let your family know where you are," Marissa stated, "in case you need us or we need you."

She held up her cell phone. "That's why I carry one of these. It goes where I go."

Jillian glanced over at Marissa. "When did you become such a worrywart?"

"Mom imposed these rules on us and so I just assumed she would follow them, as well." Marissa retrieved a bottle of water from the fridge and then headed toward the door. "I'll see you all in the morning."

As soon as Marissa arrived at work, she had a few minutes to check her email before heading into a staff meeting.

Griffin was seated at the end of the table when she entered the conference room. The only available seat was the one across from him.

"Good morning," he greeted politely.

Marissa returned the greeting.

She relaxed some when Marcus asked her a question. Marissa turned sideways in her chair to face her brother.

Jacob opened the meeting by commending everyone on their hard work. The topic then turned to the upcoming high-profile trial of Blaine Morton. They had been working on the Ponzi case for months.

"Our investigators have discovered that the asset management of Houston Douglas is nonexistent. According to Blaine Morton, he had no idea that his partner's company was one huge lie," Griffin stated. "I believe him."

"Houston took investors for almost fifty billion dollars over the course of ten years," Jake interjected. "He fled the country last year, months before the authorities could build a case."

"Do we know where to find him?" Jacob questioned.

Jake shook his head. "No idea, but I'd guess that wherever he's living, there are no extradition laws."

Marissa was finding this case an interesting one. She had been looking forward to working a high-profile case like this one day and proving herself.

"One reason that Houston was so successful in fooling everyone including Morton was that he was a highly respected, well-established and esteemed financial expert," Griffin explained. "What's more, at the same time he was running his scheme, he was also running a legitimate business. He earned our client's trust because whenever they requested a withdrawal, his partner's investment company got money to them promptly. He did not tempt investors with unbelievable returns, and he reported moderate returns to his investors."

"So our defense is that Blaine Morton is also a victim," Jillian stated.

Jake and Griffin both nodded.

"This whole ordeal has wrecked his marriage and has left him bankrupt. Morton truly believed he was partnering with a legitimate company," Jake said.

"It's a good defense," Albert commented. "Let's hope the jury buys it."

"They won't if it's not the truth," Jillian contributed. "I'm not necessarily convinced that Morton had absolutely no knowledge of what was going on. I do believe his partner left him behind to face the charges. I'm just not sure I'm buying the whole ignorance-of-the-truth scenario."

Jacob looked at Marissa and asked, "What are your thoughts?"

"I feel the same way as Jillian," she responded. "The evidence we present has to be solid in order to prove our client's innocent of the charges. People, charities and other companies lost a lot of money in this scheme. They want someone's blood in return."

"I agree with my sisters," Marcus said. "There are eight hundred victims and we have to convince them and the public that this man who has dedicated his life to creating an air of respectability did not do it to defraud people into parting with their money."

As the associates debated the case, Marissa felt the tiny hairs on the back of her neck stand up. Her eyes traveled around the table till she found Harper watching her.

When his father spoke up, Harper's expression changed. He looked furious.

The meeting ended an hour later and Marissa walked with Harper to his office.

"I can tell that you're really having a hard time with this secret we're carrying," she told him as soon as she shut the door behind her. "My mom keeps asking me what's wrong, but there is nothing I can tell her."

"Marissa, my father used to be my hero," Harper said. "I wanted to be just like him. Now I don't want anything to do with him."

"I feel the same way," Marissa confessed to her cousin. "I will never look at my mother in the same way. To be completely honest, Harper, I'm not sure I can ever forgive her."

Chapter 9

There was one other car in the parking deck when Griffin arrived shortly after six o'clock the next morning. He pulled into the space designated for him and turned off the car.

Humming softly, Griffin got out and walked briskly through the front doors of the building. He had stopped off at Starbucks for a cup of his favorite coffee.

He was always grateful to have this time alone. It gave him time to sort out his day without any distraction.

"I thought I would find you here," Albert said with a small chuckle as he entered Griffin's office. "You certainly remind me of myself when I was your age. I had that same hunger…that same drive. Just like you, I used to be the first one here."

Griffin considered his words a compliment and smiled. "This is the best part of the day."

Albert nodded. "I certainly appreciate it. The quiet."

They talked for a few minutes more before Albert left and headed to his corner office down the hall.

Griffin turned his focus to a case he was working on that would be going to trial next week, but he was finding it difficult to concentrate. He could not stop thinking about Marissa. Everything about the firm, including his office, reminded him of her.

Griffin found himself tortured by the images of that one night they had spent together. He regretted giving in so easily to his impulses. Griffin knew that Marissa felt the same way because of the gulf between them now. They used to be so close before that night. There were moments when Marissa seemed to condemn him with her eyes, although she tried to hide her true feelings.

It was his fault really. He had come up with the stupid idea that they act as if nothing had happened between them—as if he were capable of forgetting the most incredible night of his life.

Making love to Marissa had been wonderful.

Griffin debated whether he should attempt to have an honest conversation with Marissa about that night. Perhaps it might help to clear the air. On second thought, it might make things worse, he decided.

Outside in the halls he heard voices. Employees were starting to arrive for work.

Griffin returned his attention to a case that would soon go to trial. He was grateful that this one seemed to be an easy win for the firm. This would leave him with more time to prepare for the upcoming Morton trial.

He knew the moment Marissa arrived because he felt her presence. Griffin was tempted to leave his office just to get a glimpse of her beautiful smile, but to do so would be more than a mistake. It would be his undoing.

Marissa had been in her office for all of thirty minutes when she suddenly felt completely overwhelmed.

"What am I doing here?" she whispered.

She loved being a lawyer, but there were times when she questioned her decision to become one. Was it because everyone in her family seemed to follow family tradition? Was it because it was expected of her?

Marissa eyed the stack of paperwork on her desk and sighed. Although she had gotten a full night's sleep, she was still battling exhaustion. Now that her nausea was dissipating, she was back to working longer hours to stay on top of her workload.

She wanted to prove to her family for the last time that she could handle her job, especially now that she was having a baby.

Marissa thought about the way she had questioned her mother the night before. Things would never be the same between them because she no longer trusted Jeanette.

She had enough on her plate in both her personal and professional life. Marissa got up and walked over to the window, peering out.

I have to find a way to deal with this stuff. I can't let myself become stressed out.

Her assistant knocked softly on the door before strolling inside.

"Here is the information you requested for the Hanover case," she told Marissa. "It just came over on the fax."

"Thank you, Roberta."

When the telephone rang, Roberta leaned over the desk and answered it. "Marissa Hamilton's office. Oh, hello, Mrs. Hamilton. How are you?"

Marissa tensed. Her mother was on the telephone.

I don't want to talk to her right now.

"It was so nice talking to you, Mrs. Hamilton. Marissa's right here," Roberta said.

Marissa made her way back to her desk. She took the phone from her assistant and waited until Roberta had exited. "Hello, Mother."

"I hope I haven't interrupted anything important," Jeanette said.

"I can take a few minutes."

"Marissa, I wanted to know if we could have lunch. I feel like we're growing apart."

"I'm really busy today," she responded abruptly. "There is a lot going on here in the office, as I'm sure Daddy's already told you."

"Your father will understand—"

"Mother, please stop trying so hard," Marissa snapped. "None of this has anything to do with you. I am just really trying to stay focused."

Jeanette was silent for a moment.

"Mother…"

"I'll let you get back to your work."

Marissa hung up the phone and wiped away a tear.

The tears would not stop coming. She had not shown much emotion since finding out about her mother's affair. But this, on top of work, being pregnant and feeling alone, was just too much. She let out a sob and released all that she had kept locked away as she cried.

* * *

It was time he and Marissa had a conversation.

Griffin decided that they both needed closure about that night. He rose from his desk and strolled briskly out of his office. They could not continue working together with a cloud of tension floating over their heads. It followed them everywhere, and soon others in the office would begin to notice.

He navigated to the other side of the floor where Marissa's office was located. Griffin opened the door and entered without knocking.

Marissa quickly wiped her eyes with her hands, but not quick enough to keep him from seeing her tears.

"This is not a good time, Griff," she managed to say.

"I can see that," he said. "What's wrong, Marissa?"

She wiped her face with the back of her hand. "Would you do me a favor and please leave? I need some time alone."

Instead, he sat down in one of the chairs facing her desk. He would not hear of leaving her like this. "You know, I used to be the one you came to whenever you had any problems. Marissa, what happened to us?"

She bristled at his words. "That was then, Griff," Marissa stated flatly. "I'm surprised you would ask me that, especially when you were the one who said that going forward we needed to keep our distance."

Suddenly it dawned on Griffin that *he* might be the reason behind her tears. "Marissa, I'm so sorry. I really messed up everything."

She stared down at her keyboard. "There's really no need to apologize. We are both adults and we knew what we were doing."

"I want you to know that I really miss our friendship."

Marissa looked up at him. "You set the terms, Griff."

"I didn't expect that we would become so distant," Griffin admitted. He had hoped they would be able to remain friends, but Marissa did not seem interested in having him as a friend.

"You said we should keep our distance and that's what I did. I don't know what else you expect me to do." Marissa released a sigh. "Griff, I really don't want to continue this discussion. What's done is done. We cannot go back and change what happened that night. We can only move forward, and this is exactly what I plan to do. Now, if you would please excuse me…"

Griffin nodded. "For the record, I do care for you, Marissa."

She did not respond.

Confused, Griffin headed back to his office. He was not sure what to make of Marissa's lack of response.

He removed his blazer and hung it up in the narrow closet and then navigated over to his desk and sat down to check his email.

He had been invited to speak to a group of law students at Beasley School of Law at Temple University. Griffin quickly checked his calendar and accepted the invitation.

An image of Marissa formed in his mind. Griffin shook his head as if trying to shake her from his thoughts. He put a hand to his mouth, disconcerted.

Griffin tried to regain his focus. He pushed away from his desk and got up. He walked to the door of his office. "Paula, could you come here, please?"

His assistant immediately responded by saying, "I'll be right there."

Griffin walked back over to his desk and sat down.

Paula rushed in. "I have those papers you needed," she announced. "Oh, and I will be meeting with Mr. Drake this afternoon."

He nodded. "Come get me afterward. I want to talk to him."

"Will do."

It had shaken Griffin to see Marissa crying in her office. It only served to make him feel worse. He hoped that she would one day be able to forgive him. Maybe in time, she would lock it away in the back of her mind.

For Griffin, it would not be so easy.

Chapter 10

Marissa was deep in thought.

Her brief conversation with Griffin had left her with mixed emotions. Instead of saying that he was sorry for turning her away, Griffin only seemed sorry that they crossed that professional line because their working relationship was now strained.

Marissa had hoped that he would confess having feelings for her, but apparently, she had misread him.

He is not in love with me.

She sighed in resignation. "There's no turning back now," she whispered. "It's just you and me, little one. When the case doesn't go your way, you just keep moving forward—that's the first thing I learned in law school."

For the moment, her pregnancy was the least of her worries. They were preparing for the Ponzi-scheme case that would go to trial in a few weeks. Marissa had been reading about the victims in the news and heard them on the radio and television. For many of them, nailing Blaine Morton would be a catharsis of sorts. Blaine was the subject of extreme public scorn. This would not be an easy case to win.

Although she knew that she needed to tell Griffin about the baby, there was never a perfect time. He was busy assisting Jake and Harper with this case. Everyone, including Marissa, noticed how distracted Harper had become. She was the only one who knew the reason behind his distraction.

Marissa called Harper.

"Have lunch with me," she said when he answered the phone.

"Can we do it now?" he asked.

"Sure. I'll meet you at the elevator."

They left the building and walked across the street.

Inside the restaurant, Marissa told him, "Harper, I know you're hurt by Uncle Frank's actions, but you can't let this affect your work. You've got a huge case to prepare for, and the firm is counting on you."

He met Marissa's gaze. "Do you think I really care? The Hamiltons are just a bunch of pretenders. That photo shoot we did for your mother two months ago— those pictures are a bunch of lies to defraud people into thinking we're something that we're not. A *family.*"

"Harper, we are still a family," Marissa said. "No family is perfect, and just like any other family in the world, we have our problems."

"Is it that simple for you?" he asked. "Have you forgiven your mother?"

"No, but I am not going to let it take over my life.

Harper, instead of being angry, why don't you put that energy into working this case?"

He appeared to be silently considering her words.

They made small talk while they ate.

Marissa was thrilled when she was finally awarded a smile from Harper. The strain of what he knew was too much for her cousin.

"I forgot that you were also on the board," Marissa said when Griffin sat down beside her at a luncheon to benefit orphans.

"I was the one that told you about it, remember?" he responded.

After the event, they joined the other members for a tour of the orphanage.

Marissa smiled as she watched Griffin interact with the children. He would make a good father, she thought silently.

"You're very good with them," she said when he joined her.

"I love children," Griffin said. "How about you? Do you want kids someday?"

His question startled Marissa. "S-sure," she said softly.

Griffin's gaze was so intense that she searched for an escape. Marissa found it when they neared a women's bathroom. "Excuse me."

I need to tell him about the baby. Should I just blurt it out?

No, she decided. The timing had to be perfect.

Marissa placed a hand on her belly. "I am going to tell him soon, little one."

Griffin was waiting for her when she walked out of the bathroom. "You didn't have to wait for me."

"I didn't mind," he told her.

They left for the office after the tour.

Griffin escorted Marissa to her car, telling her about his invitation to speak at Temple.

She smiled at him. "That's wonderful, Griffin." She really was happy for him, the way she'd be happy for any friend.

But as she climbed into her car and closed the door, she knew that she and Griffin could never be just "friends." She cared too much for him. However, they would have to find a way to coparent if he wanted to be a part of his child's life.

She decided that she needed to also try to mend her relationship with her mother. Like with Harper, the secret of her mother's affair was weighing heavily on her.

That evening, she decided to surprise her family with dinner.

Marissa eyed the dining-room table and smiled. She had scented candles stationed in the center of the table.

Humming softly, Marissa strolled into the kitchen to see how her meal was faring. The roast chicken and scalloped potatoes smelled delicious.

She left the kitchen and went upstairs to put on a black, long-sleeved maxi-dress. She then slipped on a pair of black flats.

Her mother arrived thirty minutes later.

"Something smells good," Jeanette said with a smile.

"Thank you," Marissa said. "I thought I'd make us some dinner. Everything should be ready soon."

Her father arrived with a beautiful bouquet of flowers for Jeanette.

"These are for you," Jacob said, holding out the flowers to her. "When I saw them, they reminded me of you."

She sniffed the colorful bouquet and said, "They're beautiful, Jacob. Thank you."

Marissa turned away and continued what she was doing.

Jillian arrived a few minutes later. "Those flowers are beautiful, Mother," she said. "What are we celebrating?"

"Family," Jeanette murmured with a smile. "Marissa cooked a wonderful dinner for us. I think we should sit down and just enjoy this evening together. It's been a while since we've done this."

They all sat down at the mahogany dining table to eat as soon as the food was ready.

Jacob quickly blessed the food before they dived in.

"Marissa, I really appreciate the effort you put into this," her mother said.

"Thanks, Mother," she said. "I know that I've been focusing a lot on work and I…well, I thought I should make some time for us."

Marissa could feel her father watching her. She would not look in his direction for fear that he could read the truth in her eyes. She was struggling to keep the feelings of betrayal at bay. She wiped her mouth with the edge of her napkin.

Jillian stuck a forkful of food into her mouth and chewed slowly. "This is really delicious. Marissa, you're a wonderful cook."

She smiled. "Thank you."

"Maybe you should give it a try, Jillian," their father said.

"Funny, Dad."

Marissa chuckled. "Practice makes perfect."

Laughter rang out around the table.

It had been a while since they were able to laugh like this.

After they finished eating, Marissa pushed away from the table and stood up. "I'm going to clean up the kitchen."

"I'll help," Jillian offered.

Marissa looked at her sister in disbelief. "Really? *You?*"

They put the dishes into the dishwasher and put away the rest of the food. When the kitchen was clean, they settled down in the family room with their parents to watch a movie together.

Marissa discreetly watched as her parents interacted with each other. They seemed so in love.

Was it just an illusion? she wondered.

Marissa shook her head. She wanted to rid herself of those thoughts because they would only feed her anger and disappointment. She was trying to work through her feelings. It was best for her family.

Marissa eased inside the lecture room to listen as Griffin talked about his path to becoming an associate with Hamilton, Hamilton and Clark.

"The journey was a difficult one at times," Griffin told the audience. "But not impossible. It's the same for all of you."

He was an eloquent speaker. Marissa enjoyed listening to him.

She smiled when she spied a couple of female students whispering about him. Griffin was extremely handsome and Marissa understood completely why they were fawning over him. He still had a way of astounding her whenever they were in the same room.

As he neared the end of his speech, Marissa stood up and made her way to the exit doors. She did not want Griffin to know that she had come.

She could hear the entire room explode in applause.

Marissa wiped away her tears. They were not sad tears, but happy ones. She was thrilled for Griffin. All of his dreams were coming true.

She had no idea how her news was going to affect him, but it was time that he knew about the baby. He had a right to know before anyone else figured out that she was pregnant.

Chapter 11

Marissa decided to wait until everyone had left the office before approaching Griffin. She found him in his office working. He had loosened his tie and rolled up the sleeves of his shirt. She quietly surveyed him for a moment. He was so handsome, even now when he was focused on whatever currently held his attention.

He must have sensed her presence and looked up. "What are you still doing here?"

"I needed to talk to you," she said, walking into the office. "Do you have a moment?"

Griffin nodded. "I was just about to call it a night. What's going on?"

Marissa sat down in one of the visitor chairs. "You did a great job earlier today."

He frowned. "What are you talking about?"

"When you were speaking to the law students," Marissa said. "I went to Temple. I wanted to hear your talk."

Griffin's eyes widened in surprise. "Why didn't you say something to me?"

Marissa gave a slight shrug. "I don't know. Things have been a little crazy between us for a while," she began. "Some of it has to do with you, but not all of it."

She sighed. "Griff, I found out something about my family that is really disturbing. Honestly, it is just about the worst thing I could ever imagine. However, what is even worse than the secret itself is the fact that the people I trusted most lied to me."

Marissa glanced up at Griffin. "And I'm not going to do that to you. I owe you the truth. There is something that I need to tell you."

"I'm listening," Griffin murmured, although he looked very confused. "Does it have anything to do with this secret you mentioned?"

Marissa shook her head. "No, Griff. That secret can wait, but this cannot." She inhaled deeply, and then exhaled slowly. Gathering up her courage, she announced, "I'm pregnant."

She heard his quick intake of breath, but when Griffin did not immediately respond, Marissa continued, "*You and I* are going to have a baby."

A long moment of silence passed before Griffin seemed to register what she said.

"But you can't be!" Griffin blurted. "Marissa, we used protection. It can't be. That night…"

"We conceived a child," Marissa finished for him when the shock he was feeling seemed to silence him.

It certainly was not the joyous reaction Marissa secretly hoped for.

"Are you sure?"

She nodded. "I'm in my sixteenth week."

At this, his expression changed from shock to anger. "You've known all this time and didn't think of telling *me?*"

"Believe me, I've thought of nothing else, Griff. I wanted to tell you as soon as I found out, but then I remembered our conversation.... You made it clear that we couldn't have a relationship." Marissa met his gaze. "I didn't want you to feel obligated."

"I can't believe that you think so little of me," he stated with an angry shake of his head.

"Griff, it's not like that at all," Marissa countered. "The last thing I wanted was you feeling trapped. Neither one of us planned for something like this to happen."

"So you think I can just walk away from you and the child we created?" Griffin shook his head. "I will start making arrangements at once."

"Arrangements for what?" Marissa demanded in a harsh tone. "If you think I'm about to have an abortion, you're—"

Griffin interrupted her with a short laugh filled with little humor. "You really don't know me at all, Marissa."

"Then what arrangements are you talking about? I'm not about to give my baby up for adoption either."

"Marissa, I am referring to wedding plans," Griffin announced as calmly as he could manage. "We have to get married—the sooner the better."

Marissa silently studied Griffin a moment before uttering, "You can't be serious."

His sudden proposal was better than suggesting an abortion or adoption, but the grim expression on his face decimated whatever happiness she might have felt.

"You really cannot be serious about getting married," Marissa stated as a wave of shock flowed through her body. They had never even been on a real date, and now Griffin was talking marriage.

"I am very serious."

She gave him a sidelong glance of utter disbelief. "I'm sure you may think this is the right thing to do, Griff, but I do not intend to get married just because I'm pregnant. This baby and I deserve much more than your feeling obligated to do the right thing."

Marissa remembered all too well how quickly Griffin had tossed away their relationship for the sake of his career.

"Marissa, this baby deserves to be raised by both parents."

"I agree," she said. "But I don't want my child to grow up with parents who don't love each other. Griff, we can coparent without getting married. People do it all of the time."

"That's fine for some folk, but I don't want that for a child of mine, Marissa."

"And I don't want a marriage of convenience either," she said.

"We have to put this child first."

Marissa nodded in agreement. "Yes, we do, but Griff, I know what I can live with and what I cannot."

"Would it be so terrible being married to me?" he asked.

"No," she answered softly. "You're a good man, Griff, but…"

"I do care about you, Marissa."

"But is it enough to build a marriage on?" She wanted to know. Marissa was in love with Griffin and she wanted nothing more than to spend the rest of her life with him, but she could clearly see that he did not share those feelings.

"Isn't our child worth the risk of trying?"

Marissa did not know how to respond to his question. She and Griffin wanted the same thing for their child—the chance to grow up with both parents—but she could not bear being married to a man who did not love her.

"I am not going to allow you to shut me out of my child's life, Marissa." Griffin's tone was adamant. He was still struggling with the news that they had conceived a child together. How could she have kept this news from him all this time?

"Why did you wait until now to tell me?" he asked.

"I wanted to get through the first trimester," she responded. "I didn't want to disrupt your life and end up miscarrying."

Griffin pushed away from his desk and rose to his feet. He walked over to where she sat. "Marissa, you should have come to me. You didn't have to deal with this all alone."

She glanced up at him. "Griff, you made a decision about us five months ago."

He pulled her to her feet and then placed a hand

gently to her stomach. "This baby changes everything for me."

A myriad of emotions swamped him, and strange sensations overtook him. He looked up from her stomach and met her eyes. "I—" He was about to speak, but he heard her father's voice in the hallway.

"What is he doing back here?" she whispered.

At the sound of a knock on her door, Marissa quickly stepped away from Griffin, saying, "We'll finish this later."

"Indeed," he murmured.

Griffin opened the door and stepped aside to allow Jacob entrance.

"I stopped by your office earlier," Jacob told Marissa.

"I needed to go over something with Griffin," she managed to say. "Did you need to speak to me?"

"I'll come by shortly," Jacob said. "Right now I need to talk to Griffin."

She excused herself and slowly made her way to the door. Marissa paused for a brief second to gaze at Griffin, who gave her a tight smile.

Griffin felt a momentary panic. *How will Jacob react when he finds out that his baby girl is pregnant and I am the father? I'll probably be out looking for another job,* he thought miserably. *That is, if Jacob doesn't demand my head on a platter.*

Chapter 12

The next day, Marissa expected to see Griffin standing in her office by the time she arrived, but was disappointed when she found it empty. He'd called her last night after leaving the office, but Marissa did not want to finish their discussion over the telephone.

She sat down at her desk for a few minutes before a knock at her door drew her attention.

"Daddy, what are you doing here?" she asked when he entered her office. "I thought you were going to spend the day with Mother."

"I had forgotten that Albert and I were having lunch today with a potential client," Jacob responded, "until he called me."

A wave of nausea hit Marissa unexpectedly. She had thought those days were over.

She clamped a hand to her mouth and closed her eyes, silently praying that she would not embarrass herself.

Jacob was instantly concerned. "Marissa, are you feeling okay? Your mother mentioned that you have not been looking quite yourself. Maybe you should take the rest of the day off."

She shook her head. "I'll be fine, Daddy."

Marissa secretly felt like leaving, but decided against it, as she did not want the other employees to think that she received special treatment from her father.

"Sweetheart, I agree with your mother. You do not look well. Go home and get some rest. All of this will be here tomorrow and the day after that."

Marissa considered her father's suggestion. She was still feeling a bit nauseated and unsettled. Although she and Griffin needed to finish their conversation, Marissa did not feel up to it today. Their conversation had left her with much to think about.

Griffin walked by her office just as Marissa stepped into the hallway, her father on her heels. She did not have a chance to let him know that she was leaving for the rest of the day because her father whisked Griffin away.

Just then her uncle walked out of a conference room. Marissa used to adore her uncle Frank, but now…she was not sure what she felt about him.

"Marissa, how are you?" Frank inquired.

"I'm fine," she responded dryly.

His brows rose in surprise. "Hey, what's wrong?"

"Nothing's wrong," Marissa lied. "I have my dream job and I'm keeping busy. What could possibly be wrong?"

Her uncle did not look convinced. "You sure? I've

never known you to act so distant before. You and I—
we have always been pretty close."

*That was before I knew about your affair with my
mother.*

She nodded. "See you later, Uncle Frank."

*Uncle... What if he is my biological father? He can't
be. It just can't be true.*

Jeanette was home on the phone with a caterer iron-
ing out the final details for the charity gala.

Marissa waved at her and then went upstairs to her
bedroom.

She lay in her bed thinking back over her childhood.

*Was my mother unhappy? Did my parents fight? And
what about Uncle Frank and Aunt Vanessa?*

Marissa racked her brain looking for signs that gave
credence to Harper's claims. But all she remembered
was a blissfully happy childhood, growing up feeling
secure and loved.

*What if it was all a lie? What if my parents don't really
love each other?*

That thought scared her more than anything.

What am I going to do about Griff?

The question remained on her mind even as she fell
asleep.

The telephone rang, waking her.

It was Jillian.

"I heard that you went home sick," she said. "Do you
need me to bring you anything home?"

"No, I'm feeling much better now. I think I was just
really tired."

"Marissa, I hope you're not pushing yourself too

hard," Jillian said. "I know how much you want to prove yourself to Daddy."

"I'm not," Marissa said. "I'll be fine."

"Well, call me if you need anything."

Marissa smiled. "Thanks for calling, Jillian."

She hung up and then lay back down. She had not realized just how exhausted she was until she came home and got in bed. Marissa knew that some of what she was feeling had to do with stress. She was going to have to make some lifestyle changes, she decided. For the sake of her child.

An hour later, she climbed out of bed and went downstairs to make a salad.

Her mother had left a note saying that she had gone to the club for a late lunch with her friend Estelle.

Marissa was surprised when the doorbell sounded. She wasn't expecting company and was pretty sure that Jeanette hadn't planned on any.

Marissa was even more surprised to find Griffin standing there when she opened the front door.

"I heard that you were sick," he said.

"I'm feeling better," she told him. "There is no need for you to worry about me."

Griffin glanced around. "Are you alone?"

She nodded. "I suppose you came here so that we could finish our conversation."

"I'd like to do so, if you feel up to it," Griffin admitted. "If you're not well, we can do it another time."

Marissa gestured for him to follow her. "Come into the kitchen. I just made some lunch."

Griffin walked into the kitchen with Marissa. He sat down at the breakfast table.

"Are you hungry?" she asked. "There's more than enough for the two of us."

"I'm fine," he assured her.

Marissa carried her plate to the table and sat down facing him. "Griff, I'm sorry I didn't tell you about the baby sooner. I just thought it was best to wait."

"I don't agree," he countered. "This concerns both of us—not just you, Marissa. You really should have told me about the baby as soon as you found out."

"Why?" she asked "Were you going to suggest that I have an abortion? Are you upset because it's too late to terminate the pregnancy?"

His eyes flashed in anger. "I told you before that I would never consider aborting my child."

"I considered it," Marissa confessed. "I panicked when I first found out, but then I realized that I could never terminate this child."

Griffin seemed to sag with relief. "You didn't have to go through this alone, Marissa. That's why I wished you'd come to me. We could have… Anyway, it is done, and we can't go back."

"Griff, I don't want to rush into any decisions right now. There is so much going on in my life."

"You can't keep this pregnancy a secret much longer, Marissa."

She glanced down at her belly. "I know."

"We have to have some kind of plan."

Griffin was right. They needed to have something in place. Her family would want to know how they were going to handle this situation. Marriage seemed to be the best solution, because Marissa knew that her mother cared what others would say about her pregnant unmarried daughter.

"I should talk to your father."

"About what?" Marissa asked. "The baby?"

"He needs to know before someone else figures out the truth and tells him."

"No," Marissa said. "*We* will tell him when the time is right."

"And when will that be?" Griffin asked.

Marissa gave a slight shrug. "I don't know, but just don't say anything for right now. Please, Griff."

He reached over and took her hand in his. "We have to tell your parents soon. You won't be alone in this. I will be right there beside you."

Marissa scanned his face. "I know that you're afraid that you're going to lose your job. Griff, I won't let Daddy fire you. He can't."

"It's his company. He can do as he pleases."

"He won't fire you, Griff. I promise you." She was quiet for a moment and then said, "Now I get it. That's why you want to marry me. You want to keep your job."

"You're wrong," Griff said. "I want to marry you so that our child will have a family."

She shook her head. "No, I'm not. You are only trying to stay on course for making partner."

"I care about you, Marissa," Griffin stated loudly. "I thought you knew that."

"You find me attractive—that's all."

He looked frustrated. "Marissa, I can't get you out of my mind. You infiltrate my thoughts at the most inconvenient times. When I'm preparing for a case...when I'm trying to focus..."

She met Griffin's gaze. "You never told me any of this."

"That's because I tried to fight my feelings for you. I kept telling myself that this was the time to focus on my career. Time for love would come later. That night has changed everything, Marissa."

"Griff, I had those same dreams, and you're right—this baby changes things to a degree. But we can still have what we've dreamed."

"We have to put this child first and that means that we have to work on being a family. I don't want to wait until after the child is born," Griffin stated. "I want our family established before he or she is born."

"My mind is made up, Griff. I will not marry someone without love."

He was going to be a father.

Griffin repeated it over and over in his head. He and Marissa were going to be parents.

He loved children and he wanted to have a family, but he had not considered that it would come as soon as it had.

He *was* in love with Marissa, but how could he convince her that his feelings were real—that his wanting to marry her had nothing to do with keeping his job? Griffin knew that he was a good attorney. He would not have a hard time landing employment with another firm. Recruiters contacted him weekly to see if he was interested in moving to another company.

Griffin knew that Marissa had feelings for him, as well. However, he did not understand why she did not trust him. She kept mentioning some secret about her family. He had been so focused on the baby that he had not questioned her further on the subject.

He was determined to find a way to get Marissa to trust him again. *I'm not going to lose my family,* he vowed.

Griffin sat down to watch television but could not concentrate. His mind stayed on Marissa and the child she carried.

She looked so beautiful, her healthy complexion clear of blemishes. She no longer looked pale as she did in the weeks past. Griffin had been concerned that she was working too hard and making herself ill.

He felt foolish now for not recognizing the weight gain and the sickness that seemed to disappear as the day wore on. Perhaps it was because of the distance between them. Griffin wanted to think that he would have noticed sooner, but he could not be sure. Her own family had no idea that she was pregnant.

Griffin thought about her brothers Jake, Anthony and Marcus. He worked closely with them and wondered how they would react. It did not matter, because their feelings would not change anything. He and Marissa were still going to have a baby together.

He still cared how Jacob would react, but Griffin decided to take it one day at a time.

First he had to convince Marissa of his love for her and their child.

Chapter 13

Over the next several days, Griffin had Marissa work with him as he prepared for trial. They were seated in the conference room along with Harper and Jillian.

"One of Morton's victims just filed a suit against him," Jake announced as he strolled into the room. He sat down at the head of the table. "This is going to be the first of many, I have a feeling."

Jillian agreed.

Marissa silently noted how tired her brother looked. Jake, Harper and Griffin had been pulling longer hours than usual as they prepared to defend Morton. Even Griffin's eyes sagged with exhaustion.

"The feds are going after Houston," Griffin stated before stifling a yawn. "He had a heart attack over the weekend and is in a hospital in Costa Rica. They are trying to get him extradited upon his release."

"I hope they can get him here in enough time to turn

this around for Morton." Jake picked up a legal document, scanning it. "We need Houston to confess his part in all this and how he defrauded Morton, as well."

"The district attorney wants to charge Morton's wife," Harper announced. "She was picked up at the airport with a bag of money and trying to board a plane to Mexico."

Griffin groaned. "What is this woman doing?"

"What is the charge?" Jake wanted to know.

"Something about unjust enrichment under Pennsylvania law," Harper explained. "It's a crock."

"She started divorce proceedings against Morton last month," Griffin stated. "The media are going to have a field day with this."

"I thought she was going to stay with Morton at least until the trial was over," Jillian said. "You know, the whole united front."

Harper shrugged. "Apparently, Mrs. Morton has changed her mind. She's probably tired of living a lie."

Marissa glanced over at her cousin.

She was grateful when Blaine Morton walked into the conference room.

Griffin rose to his feet and said, "Mr. Morton, thank you for coming. We need to discuss the trial."

Marissa surveyed their client. Blaine Morton looked nothing like the monster the media made him out to be. The bags under his eyes showed that he had not been sleeping well, if at all. There was a sickly pallor to his complexion.

"I understand why clients hate me," he said. "They think that I ruined their lives and lived off their hard-earned money. I had no idea that Houston was swindling our investors of billions of dollars. I didn't know. I trusted the man."

Marissa listened as Jake explained the trial process to Morton.

When the subject of his wife came up, Morton said, "She asked me to let her go. She does not deserve any of this. She has changed the home phone number six times, but people keep finding out the new number. I no longer live at the house, but still they call and harass her. It's not right."

Marissa felt sorry for Morton. He seemed weary emotionally and physically. Blaine looked as if it was a struggle just to breathe. The ordeal had clearly taken a toll on him.

After their meeting with Morton ended, Griffin's assistant brought in a tray of sandwiches.

"I noticed that you haven't eaten anything," Griffin whispered as he sat down beside Marissa.

"I'm not hungry," she said softly. Marissa's gaze bounced around the room to see if anyone was paying attention to her and Griffin. She hoped that he would just take a seat and drop the "concerned" act altogether.

"Marissa, you have to put something in your stomach."

She shook her head. "I can't right now."

Griffin grew alarmed. "Are you feeling sick?"

She sent him a sharp glare. "Griff, keep your voice down. We can't talk about this right now."

Marissa pushed away from the table and walked away briskly. She returned to her seat a few minutes later with a bottle of water. She opened her planner and pretended to go over her schedule.

She could feel the heat of Griffin's gaze on her.

Although he seemed concerned for her health, Marissa could tell that he was angry with her for keeping the pregnancy a secret. She had done what she thought was best at the time and hopefully, one day he would understand.

He wanted to get married.

But he did not love her. She believed that he cared for her, but Griffin was not in love with her.

Marissa did not want a marriage in name only, and there would be no compromise.

"Knock…knock…"

"Jillian," Griffin greeted politely. He had no idea why she had come by his office to see him, but judging by the expression on her face, this had something to do with Marissa. He knew how close the Hamilton siblings were and they were also very protective of one another. Griffin leaned back in his chair, his eyes never leaving Jillian's face.

She closed the door behind her so that their conversation would not be overheard. "I need to talk to you," Jillian said. "About my sister."

Griffin was instantly on guard. Had Marissa confided in her sister? He did not think so, because they had discussed keeping the pregnancy just between the two of them for now.

Jillian sat down in one of the visitor chairs facing him. "What's going on between you and Marissa?"

He was careful to keep his expression blank. "What are you talking about, Jillian?"

Griffin could tell that Jillian was not buying his "dumb" act.

"Something is going on, Griff," she stated flatly. "I could practically see the tension in the air between you two earlier—it was that thick. Marissa hasn't dated much, you know. I can't stand by and let you hurt my sister."

He settled back in his chair. "Jillian, I think this is a conversation you should be having with your sister."

"Why is that?" she asked.

"If there is anything Marissa wants to share with you, she should be the one to do it," Griffin responded.

Jillian met his gaze without blinking. "I'm going to say this again, Griff. I do not want to see my sister get hurt."

"Neither do I," he told her.

"Then you'd better see that she doesn't get hurt." Jillian rose to her feet. "Marissa is still young and—"

Griffin interrupted her. "Your sister is a very beautiful and intelligent woman, Jillian. Marissa is not a little girl and she knows exactly what she wants."

She inclined her head. "You seem to know an awful lot about my sister."

"We work together and I am her mentor, Jillian. I'd like to think that Marissa and I are also friends."

Jillian shook her head. "Nooo…I have a feeling that it's a whole lot more than friendship going on between you and Marissa. You just better not hurt her."

The damage has already been done, Griffin thought.

Marissa was glad to have the huge house all to herself. Her father was at a business function, her mother was either out shopping or tending to the charity-gala tasks and her sister was out with friends.

She bit into a saltine cracker.

Her stomach had settled down some, but she still felt nauseated occasionally.

She slowly made her way upstairs to her bedroom, carrying a glass of ginger ale and a pack of saltines.

She was just about to lie down when she heard someone calling out for her. Marissa released a long sigh at the sound of Jillian's voice as she made her way upstairs.

"What now?" she whispered.

Jillian entered the bedroom without knocking, which irritated Marissa. "I'm pretty sure that my door was closed." She picked up a pillow and held it in front of her, covering her stomach.

"I need to talk to you," Jillian blurted.

Marissa sat down on the edge of her bed. "About what?"

"Griff."

She swallowed hard. She couldn't help wondering if Griffin had said something to her sister. No, he wouldn't have, Marissa decided. Griffin was very private when it came to his personal life.

"Is there something going on between you and Griff?" Jillian asked. "I tried asking him, but all he would say is that I needed to talk to you."

"Why would you do something like that?" Marissa demanded. "I am not some little kid, Jillian. If there is anything between me and Griff, it's our business. Not *yours*."

"I don't want to see you get hurt," Jillian said. "I'm

not stupid, Marissa. Something must have happened between the two of you because I can see that there is some tension between you when you and Griff are in the same room."

"Regardless, it is none of your business, Jillian." She picked up the pack of saltines.

"You're not feeling well?"

Marissa gave a slight shrug. "It's nothing serious."

Jillian openly studied her. "You really don't look like yourself. Have you seen a doctor?"

Marissa's stomach roiled and she jumped up, making a fast dash to the bathroom.

After emptying the contents of her belly, Marissa washed her face and brushed her teeth. When she walked out, she found Jillian sitting on her bed, deep in thought.

"Sorry about that," she murmured.

Jillian turned to look at Marissa. Her eyes traveled from her sister's face to her belly and rested there.

"It all makes sense now," she said. "The way you've been acting, your pale complexion... You're pregnant."

Marissa glanced over at her reflection in the mirror. The oversized T-shirt and sweats did nothing to hide the roundness of her belly. Although she wanted to deny the truth, Marissa was actually relieved to be able to share her pregnancy with someone—someone who might actually be happy about it.

"I'm right, aren't I?" Jillian asked. "You're pregnant."

Marissa nodded.

"So how...who..." Her eyes widened as she murmured, "Griff..."

"Yes, Griff is the father of my baby," Marissa confirmed.

"I knew there was something between you two," Jillian said. "You wait until I see him. I—"

"Before you start blaming him for everything, don't," Marissa uttered. "Griff had no idea I was pregnant until recently. I kept it a secret from everyone including him. When I told Griff, the first thing he wanted to do was get married right away, but I turned him down."

Jillian looked surprised. "But why?"

"Because he is not in love with me," Marissa said. "I won't marry a man who doesn't love me."

"What happened between the two of you besides, you know…?"

"We were working late one night, Jillian. I have always had feelings for Griff, and one thing just led to another. Afterward…well, he decided that we'd made a huge mistake and that it would never happen again."

"Oh, he couldn't decide this before you two made love?" Jillian snapped.

"You can't just blame Griff for this," Marissa said. "We are both adults and this was a choice we made together."

"But what about protection?" Jillian asked. "Did either one of you think about that?"

Marissa nodded. "We used protection."

Her sister smiled. "Then I guess this little one is meant to be here."

"I feel the same way," Marissa said. "I already love this baby so much."

"Then maybe you shouldn't just throw away Griff's

offer of marriage," Jillian suggested. "I admire him for being willing to step up and be a husband and father."

"As much as I love him, I refuse to be viewed as some kind of obligation."

"A baby needs its father," Jillian said softly.

"I won't cut Griff out of his child's life. We will not be married, but I am sure that he and I will be able to work out an agreement."

Before her sister could comment, Marissa asked, "Jillian, what do you remember about our parents when you were growing up?"

"What do you mean?"

"Did they seem happy? Did they ever seem overwhelmed by having so many kids?"

Jillian shrugged. "They were busy, but they seemed pretty happy. I don't remember ever hearing them argue or raise their voices, even when they didn't agree on something. Why are you asking?"

"I was just curious. Ever since Griff mentioned marriage, it has been on my mind. I can't help wondering what marriage would be like—having a husband and children."

"Whoa…you are having one baby, right?" Jillian said.

Marissa laughed. "Yes, it's just one baby. One is enough for me right now."

"When do you plan to tell our parents?"

"I don't know," Marissa answered honestly. "There's so much going on right now."

Jillian pointed to her belly. "You are not going to be able to keep your pregnancy a secret much longer."

"I know." Marissa chewed on her bottom lip. "Griffin and I are going to figure out the best time to tell them."

Marissa released a short sigh. "I hate keeping secrets."

Chapter 14

Griffin paced back and forth across the hardwood floor of his apartment, his stomach full of nervous energy. *How am I going to break the news to Jacob that Marissa and I are having a baby?*

He had no idea how his boss would take the news, especially since Griffin and Marissa were not involved in a relationship.

How will he take the news of us getting married?

Griffin decided that Marissa was probably right about not rushing into marriage. He still wanted to marry her, but so far, they had done things backward. They'd conceived a child after just one night together.

We are going to be parents in a few short months, so it's time for us to investigate our feelings for each other.

Griffin wanted to explore a relationship with Marissa. He knew that his own feelings ran deep where she was concerned, but Griffin wanted to see if Marissa felt she could ever love him as much as he loved her.

He had never admitted his love for her. Griffin considered that doing so now would only make her believe that he was making the declaration because she was pregnant. He had to find a way to show her…to make Marissa feel loved. It was the only way that she would consider marrying him.

The doorbell rang, surprising him.

He opened the door to find Marissa standing there.

Griffin broke into a smile. "Come in."

He stepped aside so that she could enter.

Marissa held up a large bag. "I hope you haven't eaten dinner yet."

"I haven't," Griffin responded with a smile. "I'm glad to see you."

He took it as a good sign that she'd come to him, and he couldn't help feeling hopeful as he took out utensils and they ate right out of the Chinese food take-out containers.

They did not talk much while they ate, but every now and then Griffin would catch Marissa staring at him. It was as if she were photographing him with her eyes.

Marissa finally pushed her container away and said, "Griffin, I have to tell you something."

He wiped his mouth on the edge of a napkin before asking, "What is it?"

"Jillian came to me. She wanted to know what's going on between you and me."

"She questioned me, as well," Griffin said. "She is very protective of you, Marissa."

"My sister knows that I'm pregnant," Marissa announced. "She figured it out when she saw me in a T-shirt and sweats."

His gaze was riveted on her face. "What did she have to say?"

"She was surprised initially, but she is excited and happy for us."

"Really?" Griffin asked, not hiding his own surprise. "I figured she'd be ready to hang me without a trial."

Marissa nodded. "She just wants me to be happy."

"What if she tells your parents?"

"She won't do that," Marissa said. "Jillian will keep our secret. She has been the keeper of my secrets since I was a little girl."

"Speaking of little girls...I hope that you are carrying our daughter."

Marissa's brows raised in surprise. "I thought you would want a son."

"I do," he confessed. "But I also want a little girl."

She smiled. "I'd like a daughter also, but if this baby is a boy, I'll love him just as much."

"Pregnancy agrees with you, Marissa. You look even more beautiful each day."

"Where is all this coming from, Griff?"

He got up and walked around the table, moving toward her. He pulled her up and into his arms.

"I don't just want to be a part of our child's life. I want to be in your life, Marissa."

He held her snugly. "This feels so right to me," he whispered. "I want you to know that you're not alone. We can get through anything you're facing. We can do it together."

She leaned back to look up at him, studying his expression.

Griffin smiled then, stirring something within him.

"What?" Marissa asked.

He pulled her close and kissed her lips. When her tongue met his, he felt shivers of desire racing through him.

Marissa matched him kiss for kiss, and in no time he felt the heat they'd generated that fateful night.

"Sweetheart, I don't want to let you go," he whispered against her open mouth.

"I can't stay," Marissa whispered. "I have a yoga class."

"Should you—"

She cut Griffin off with a wave of her hand. "Exercise is good for me. I'm not going to do anything to put the baby in jeopardy."

"Do you really have to leave?" he asked.

Marissa nodded. "I'll give you a call later."

Griffin met her gaze. "Why don't you just come back here?"

"I'll think about it," she murmured.

It was taking all of his willpower to let Marissa walk out of his apartment. Griffin wanted to give in to the passion that had been building since he laid eyes on Marissa. But now was not the time. He wondered when that time would come.

Marissa called Griffin as soon as her yoga class was over. She had debated whether to go home or go back to his apartment. Her overwhelming desire to see Griffin was the deciding factor.

"Is your offer still open?" she asked.

"Yes," he responded.

"I'll see you in a few minutes."

Smiling, she turned the key in the ignition and pulled out of the gym parking lot.

Twenty minutes later, Marissa was standing at Griffin's front door.

He welcomed her back with a kiss and then they settled down in the living room.

"I'm glad you came back," Griffin said. "I have to admit that I wasn't sure that you would."

"I wasn't sure either," she admitted. "To be honest with you, Griff—I'm not real sure why I'm here."

He placed a hand on her belly. "Because of this little one and because of your feelings for me."

Marissa looked up at him.

"Let's just be real," Griffin stated. "We have feelings for each other. I want to explore those feelings. Let's try and see if we have a real future together."

"I'd like that," she confessed. "There's been so much going on with me…"

"You keep alluding to that. Did something happen to upset you?"

She nodded.

"Do you want to talk about it?" Griffin asked. "I meant what I said about being here for you."

"Harper came to me a few weeks ago and told me something that has wrecked my whole world."

"What is it, sweetheart?"

"Someone gave Azure an anonymous tip about my family. They said that my mother and my uncle had an affair."

Griffin shook his head in disbelief. "Surely, you don't believe that."

"I didn't want to believe it," Marissa stated flatly. "But Harper confronted Uncle Frank about it and he admitted that it was true. He had an affair with my mother twenty-seven years ago."

"Have you talked to your mother about this?"

"No. I just don't know what to say to her. I don't know how she could do something like this to my dad." A tear rolled down her cheek. "Griff, the worst part of this is me."

He looked confused. "What do you mean by that?"

"The affair was *twenty-seven* years ago."

Comprehension dawned on Griffin. "Naaah…you can't think that Frank Hamilton is your biological father."

"According to this tip, he is."

Griffin wrapped an arm around her, pulling her close to him. "Honey, I'm so sorry. This is a lot to have to deal with along with everything else. Why didn't you come to me?"

Marissa wiped her eyes with the back of her hand. "Because things were very tense between us, Griff. You didn't want anything to do with me."

"That's not true," he told her. "I wanted everything to do with you, but I…I was stupid."

"I'm so angry with my mother, but I've been trying to move past those feelings. I have no right to judge her."

"She wasn't honest with you," Griffin reminded her.

"I haven't been exactly honest with her either."

"Point taken," he said. "This is your mother, Marissa.

I think that you should sit down and talk to her about this. Maybe not right now, but soon."

Marissa swallowed her pain.

"I take it that you haven't told anyone else about this?" Griffin asked. "Your brothers or Jillian have no knowledge of this?"

"How could I tell them something like this?" Marissa said. "It would destroy our family. Harper and his father are barely on speaking terms. Mother and I...we are just starting to have small conversations. My mom and Aunt Vanessa barely tolerate each other. Something like this coming out would be awful."

"I'm sorry that you're having to deal with this," Griffin murmured. "It isn't good for the baby."

"That's why I'm doing yoga," Marissa explained. "It helps to relax me."

"I have something that will help take some of that stress off you, as well."

Marissa gave Griffin a sidelong glance. "What?"

"Well, first you are going to take a nice, relaxing spa bath."

She chuckled. "Is that your polite way of saying I stink?"

Griffin laughed. "Not at all. Just trust me on this, Marissa."

"Okay," she said.

She had no idea what Griffin had planned for the two of them, but she had no intention of ending up in his bed. She was not ready to take their newfound relationship to the next level just yet.

Marissa almost laughed aloud at the irony. She was

already pregnant with his child. However, she intended to use her head this time, and not her heart.

Griffin prepared a bath for Marissa.

He left the master bedroom to join her in the living room. "Ready?"

She smiled and nodded.

Griffin took her by the hand and led her into his bedroom. "I hung a robe for you in there."

"Griff…"

He placed a finger on her lips. "Trust me."

Marissa nodded and walked into the bathroom, shutting the door behind her.

While she bathed, Griffin lit a few candles in his bedroom and then turned on some relaxing music. He made sure that it played at a soothing volume. Griffin did not want the music too loud to distract Marissa. He wanted her completely relaxed.

Satisfied with the music, he quickly prepared the bed by laying a clean sheet on top of the comforter. Griffin placed a few drops of lavender oil at the top of the sheet where Marissa would lay her head. He picked up a jar off his nightstand and opened it, sprinkling rose petals all over the bed. He had purchased the items with the intent to give them to Marissa so that she could pamper herself at home, but Griffin decided to make use of the oil and petals tonight. He then placed a stack of neatly folded towels on the edge of the king-sized bed.

The night air was cool but not enough to start a fire in the fireplace. The glow from the candles added not only ambience but also warmth to the room.

Marissa walked out of the bedroom, dressed in the

robe. She stopped in her tracks, her eyes traveling the room. She glanced over at the bed, then at Griffin.

"I'm going to give you a massage," he explained.

Griffin offered her a large towel.

Marissa smiled. "Thanks."

She turned her back to him, opened the robe and slipped the towel around her. Marissa smiled to herself as she thought about her actions. Griffin had seen the very essence of her, so it was ironic that she would behave so modestly now.

When she lay facedown on the bed, he began the massage by pouring a small amount of oil into his hands. He rubbed his hands together to warm the oil.

He used slow, firm strokes on her shoulders, using gentle pulling and kneading motions. He gently kissed Marissa's neck and shoulders as he massaged them.

He continued up her neck, using the pads of his thumbs to massage her skin in a circular motion. He smiled when a soft moan escaped her lips.

He leaned down to kiss her back.

Marissa opened her mouth to say something, but he stopped her by saying, "Shhh. No talking. Just relax."

Griffin massaged her arms, fingers and palms in the same manner, relieving her body of any knotted muscles. He could actually feel the tension melting away.

He was yearning to make love to Marissa, but it was too soon. He was determined to wait until they were at a place of shared love and commitment. He had to earn Marissa's trust once more. Her mother's betrayal had destroyed everything she believed in. Griffin knew that it would take time, and he loved Marissa enough to wait.

Chapter 15

Marissa was so relaxed that she thought she would just dissolve into a puddle of water.

Griffin's touch was gentle, yet firm as he made circular motions on her thighs and legs and down to her feet.

He took one foot in his hand and massaged the sole with his thumbs in a circular and upward-sweeping motion. He did the same with the other foot.

Although they had not made love, Marissa felt an intimacy with Griffin that she had never experienced with anyone before. The way he touched her body was sensual and erotic, igniting a flame of desire that burned within her.

When Griffin lay down beside her, Marissa snuggled up against him. It was hard to put into words, but she felt a closeness that had not existed between them before.

He wrapped his arms around her. "Marissa, I hope by now that you've realized that I'm crazy about you."

She saw the heartrending tenderness of his gaze and smiled in response. "So this is not just because I'm having your baby?"

Moving closer, he shook his head and smiled. "I care for you deeply, Marissa."

Griffin kissed her, his lips more persuasive than she cared to admit.

Burying her face in his neck, Marissa felt safe—she felt as if she had come home.

She stretched. "You give great massages."

Griffin smiled. "I love seeing you like this…without the stress."

He kissed her again.

"I missed you," Griffin confessed. "I did not realize how much until recently."

"I missed you, too, but I was so angry at you, Griff."

"I deserved it."

Marissa yawned. "I felt like we had really made a connection that night, but then you announced that you just wanted us to have a professional relationship."

"I was trying to do the right thing, Marissa. I did not want to mess up our working relationship if things didn't work out between us."

Marissa kept yawning and her eyelids grew heavy. Finally she surrendered and closed her eyes.

She fell asleep with his arms holding her close to his body.

His body hungered for her, making it a challenge to lie so close beside her. It wasn't hard for him to imagine what she looked like without the towel. Griffin had memorized every inch of her body the night they made love.

"You are such an incredible woman," he whispered

softly. "I can't imagine sharing my life with anyone else, Marissa. If only I could convince you of this."

She moaned softly in her sleep but did not awaken.

Griffin closed his eyes, savoring the feel of her body pressed against his own.

When she woke, a couple of hours had passed and it was well after midnight. She sat up in bed.

Beside her Griffin asked, "What's wrong?"

"Nothing," she responded, "I just need to go home."

He met her gaze. "You don't have to leave, Marissa. I have another bedroom. I can sleep in there."

She smiled at him. "Griff, I'm not going to kick you out of your bedroom. Thank you for everything. I really enjoyed the massage."

He grinned. "Don't forget to leave a tip."

Laughing, Marissa hit him with a pillow.

She climbed out of bed and walked into the bathroom to get dressed.

"You're sure you don't want to just stay here?" Griffin questioned when she walked out a few minutes later.

"I should go home."

Later he walked Marissa out to her car. "I'll see you tomorrow."

"Yes, you will," she said.

He pulled her into his arms, kissing her.

Marissa stepped away from him. "If you keep that up, I won't be going anywhere."

Griffin broke into a grin. "You promise?"

"I have to go."

"This feels right," he told her. "You and me."

"I always thought so," Marissa said. "But you

couldn't see it. Griff, I can't help wondering if this is just about the baby."

"It's not," he told her. "Marissa, if it's the last thing I do—I am going to show you just how much you mean to me."

When she climbed into her car and drove away, Marissa whispered, "Little one, your father is an incredible man. Mommy just doesn't know what to do. I love your father, but…let's just say that things are really confusing right now, but don't you worry. Mommy is going to figure everything out."

Every moment spent around Griffin reminded Marissa of why they got together in the first place—the sexual attraction between them was powerful. However, it was not enough to build a marriage on, she constantly reminded herself.

Apparently, love was not enough either, she decided. Her father adored her mother, but it was not enough to keep her faithful. Marissa could not bear the thought of living a lie.

I'm already living one lie.

One is more than enough.

She was relieved when Griffin stopped mentioning marriage. Marissa did not want him to pressure her into making a decision. She was grateful that he had decided to just take the relationship one day at a time, although she knew that Griffin still worried that her father might retaliate by firing him. Marissa vowed that she would not let that happen.

If Griffin had to leave the firm, then she would leave with him.

The telephone rang, cutting into her thoughts. She picked it up after the third ring; apparently her assistant wasn't at her desk.

It was Griffin.

"Why aren't you working?" she asked with a chuckle.

"Trust me, I have been working," he said. "Do you have plans for tonight?"

"No," Marissa answered.

"Come to my place. I'll even cook dinner for us."

She smiled. "Really?"

"Yes. I'll even make your favorite meal."

She broke into a grin. "Garlic shrimp?" From the first time Griffin made some for her last birthday, it had become a favorite of hers. "With the bow-tie pasta?"

"Yes."

"I'll be there," Marissa told him. "I'll even bring dessert."

Smiling, she returned her attention back to the task at hand. Marissa was looking forward to spending the evening with Griffin.

She left work promptly at five and went home to shower and prepare for her evening. Griffin was expecting her at seven-thirty.

They sat in Griffin's apartment having dinner shortly after eight. "Marissa, I still think we should get married," he blurted afterward.

"No, we should not," she responded. "Griff, I know that we care about each other, but I do not want to be a part of a loveless marriage. My child deserves more than that."

Marissa loved Griffin with her entire being, but be-

cause he did not feel the same way, she refused to confess just how much she cared for him.

Griffin wiped his mouth on a napkin. "*Our* child deserves to be raised in a two-parent household."

"If those two people love each other," she interjected.
"Griff, do you realize that we have never even been on
a real date?"

"Okay, then, let's do it," Griff said. "Let's go on a
date."

Marissa chuckled as she sliced into a shrimp.

"I'm serious."

"Really? You actually want to go on a date with me?"
Marissa stuck a forkful of food into her mouth. "But
what about all that stuff you said about focusing on your
career. I know how much you want to make partner."

"The baby that you are carrying comes first," he said.
"Besides, once your dad finds out, I may not have to
worry about making partner, at least not at Hamilton,
Hamilton and Clark."

"Griff, I don't want you to feel trapped."

He met her gaze. "That's not how I feel. You didn't
get pregnant by yourself and I won't leave you to raise
my child as a single mother."

"You really are an amazing man, Griffin Jackson."

"Not amazing enough to marry, though," he said.

"Griff…"

"I'm not going to pressure you into marriage, Marissa, but I am also not going to completely give up on
the idea. I know in my heart that getting married is the
right thing to do."

Jillian and Marissa decided to take a break from their
work and have a sisters' lunch together.

"I'm so glad we did this," Marissa told Jillian. "Things have been crazy at the firm. Even though we work and live together, I feel like I've hardly seen you all week."

"How have you been feeling?"

"Much better," Marissa answered. "The morning sickness is over, finally. I'm still tired a lot, but it's not as bad as it was."

Jillian smiled. "When are you going to tell Mom and Dad? Pretty soon everyone is going to figure it out."

Marissa scanned her menu, trying to decide what she wanted to eat. "Griff and I are working on that."

The waiter came to take their order.

"Has he convinced you to marry him?" Jillian asked after he left.

Marissa shook her head. "I can't rush into something like that. But we are spending time together."

"I thought so. I heard you when you came in late the other night. Mom asked me if you were seeing someone."

Marissa did not respond at the mention of Jeanette.

"What's going on between you and Mom?"

"Nothing," she said.

Jillian shook her head. "I'm not buying it. You're upset about something."

"It's not something I'm ready to talk about, Jillian."

"She wants to make things right but doesn't know what to do."

"There is nothing she can do." Marissa took a sip of her water. "I love Mom. She and I…we are going through something and hopefully, it will all work itself out."

"I hope so," Jillian admitted.

Marissa was grateful when the food arrived. Her sister said grace, and the conversation turned from their mother to work.

After lunch, when they returned to work, Jillian walked her to her office.

"Looks like someone is definitely trying to get you to change your mind," Jillian murmured.

Marissa followed her gaze. There was a huge bouquet of flowers on her desk.

"They arrived not too long ago," Roberta told her, coming up behind them. "They are gorgeous."

Marissa walked over to them and removed the card. She smiled as she read it.

Just something to brighten your day
From the one who loves to see that beautiful smile
of yours.

Roberta looked disappointed when she did not read the card aloud.

"Well, I'm off to see if my secret admirer left anything special in my office," Jillian said with a chuckle.

Marissa made a mental note to send her sister some flowers as a show of gratitude for her support and for keeping her secret.

She closed the door to her office and then navigated over to her desk. Marissa picked up the phone and called Griffin.

"Thank you," she said in a low voice. "They're beautiful."

"You're welcome," he said. "I wanted to do something to keep that pretty smile on your face."

"It worked."

"I heard you had lunch with your sister."

"I did," she confirmed. "She asked me about Mom and why we're so distant."

"What did you tell her?"

"Just that we were going through a thing and that it would eventually work itself out."

Marissa paused a moment before continuing. "I don't think she believed me. This is hard for me, Griff. I always thought my parents had the perfect marriage."

"Trust me, Marissa. No marriage is perfect. It is work, but worth it—at least that's what my parents always say. They have been married for almost thirty-five years."

"That's wonderful, Griff."

As casually as Marissa could manage, she asked, "How would you feel if you were in my shoes? If you found out that you had been lied to your whole life?"

"Honey, it would be hard," Griffin admitted. "I would probably react in much the same way as you have."

"I really do love my mother, and I am trying to get past this."

"Marissa, you will not have closure until you and your mom sit down and talk this thing out. Hear her out."

"I don't think I'm ready for that, Griff."

"Take your time, sweetheart," he told her. "But understand that you will have to sit down and have a conversation soon. You can't just let this fester inside you, Marissa. It's not good for you or the baby."

"I know you're right."

"Whatever you decide to do, Marissa, I'm here for you. Just remember that."

"You have no idea how much this means to me. I'm so glad to be able to talk about this with someone."

Chapter 16

Early Saturday morning, Griffin decided to visit his parents, who lived in a suburb outside Philadelphia. He loved his parents deeply and tried to visit them at least twice a month.

Olive and Gerard Jackson's apartment was a stark contrast from the castlelike mansion Marissa called home. But it was full of love.

His mother greeted him with a warm embrace. "It's so good to see my baby."

Griffin laughed. "It's good to see you, too."

His father joined them in the living room.

"So, tell me," Gerard began, "how's that case progressing? The one with the Ponzi-scheme fella."

His parents both worked for Human Services, but they were always interested in his cases. "It's going okay," Griffin said as his eyes traveled the room. His high-school sports trophies were still in a tall bookshelf in the corner. Photographs decorated the walls in front and behind him. "Why don't you and Mom start looking for a house?" he suggested. "It's my gift to you both."

His mother smiled at him and said, "Son, I can't imagine living anywhere else. This apartment may be small, but we love it. This has been our home since you were in elementary school. We have lots of memories here. Good memories."

His father agreed. "You just save your money, Griff. Someday you are going to want to settle down and raise a family. Put that money aside for your family."

Griffin always came home whenever he felt the need for a reality check.

Olive surveyed his face. "What's wrong, son?"

"Nothing. I'm just glad to be here with you and Dad. I hate that I haven't been here much lately."

"We know how busy you are," his father said. "We understand."

His mother prepared lunch while Griffin helped his father make some minor repairs around the apartment.

"Dad, I don't know about this heater. Why don't you let me get you a new one? I don't want you and Mom getting sick or freezing in this apartment."

Gerard opened his mouth to respond, but Griffin held up his hand and said, "I insist. I'll have someone come out and replace this one next week."

"Thank you, son. Your mother and I appreciate it."

Later that evening, when his father went into his bedroom to do his nightly Bible reading, Olive sat down beside Griffin.

"I know my child," she said. "What's going on with you?"

Griffin could not bring himself to tell his mother that she was going to be a grandmother. It had to be done, but he just could not tell her at this moment. She would ask too many questions, and right now he really did not have any answers.

"Talk to me, Griffin."

"I did something and now I am trying to make it right," he confessed. "That's about all that I can tell you. Except that things are not quite working out as I had hoped."

"I know you, son," Olive said. "You have never been one to just do anything foolish in your entire life. There must be a good reason why you did whatever it is that you did." She paused a moment before adding, "Fight for her."

The date was everything she'd hoped it would be.

It might have been months too late, but Marissa was thoroughly enjoying her time with Griffin. They'd gone to dinner and a movie—her choice—and now she didn't want the night to end. She accepted his offer to go to his house for a while to talk.

"So, when are we going public with this romance?" he asked once they settled on the sofa.

She shrugged. "I don't know why we have to say anything about our relationship. It's not really anybody's business."

"True," he agreed. "But when you really start showing…people are going to talk and they are going to have questions."

Marissa jumped.

"What's wrong?" Griffin asked. "Is it the baby?"

She nodded. "I can feel him or her move."

Griffin placed a hand over her belly.

"Can you feel it?" she asked excitedly.

He nodded.

"Hey, little one…" Griffin murmured, leaning toward her belly.

"I didn't think you'd feel anything," Marissa told him. "Not yet anyway."

He looked up at her. "When do you go back to the doctor?"

"On Tuesday. Why?"

"I'd like to go with you," he said. "I want to share every moment of what's left with your pregnancy."

His words touched her, bringing on a thread of guilt. "I'm so sorry, Griff. I should have told you the moment I found out. I just realized how selfish I've been with this pregnancy."

He leaned in and placed a light kiss on her lips. "Let's just focus on now and the future."

She reached over and took his hand in hers. "I'm glad that I have your support, Griff. It means the world to me. I really didn't want to have to go through this experience alone."

When he wrapped an arm around her, Marissa snuggled in close to him. He rubbed her arms in a gentle caress, and she felt a delicious shudder heat her body at the touch. Desire washed over her like waves. She could not deny it—she wanted this man.

If only he could show her how much he wanted her. But Griff worried that this was not the time. Instead, he simply held her in his arms.

"I've been reading up on what to expect during your pregnancy," he told her. "Are you taking your prenatal vitamins?"

He felt Marissa's grin against his chest. "Yes, I have been."

"You need to improve on your eating habits, though," Griffin stated. "And you need to cut back on some of those long hours in the office."

"I'm not feeling nauseated anymore, so my appetite is improving, Doctor. As for work, you know we have a huge case hanging over our heads."

"I will worry about that," Griffin said. "You just focus on taking it easy and taking care of our baby."

She got quiet a moment before she said, "Griff, why didn't you tell your parents about the baby?"

"Truth?"

Marissa nodded.

"I was ashamed of the way I treated you after making love to you that night. My parents raised me to be a much better man than that. I intend to tell them long before the baby's born, but I would like to be able to say that you and I are getting married."

"I can't promise you that I will marry you before I have the baby, Griff."

He met her gaze. "You wanted the truth and I gave it to you."

"Fair enough," Marissa said. She squeezed his hand. "One day at a time, remember?"

Griffin smiled and nodded. He loved her dearly.

Tell her, a voice inside him urged.

Marissa was already dealing with so much. Griffin decided to keep his feelings to himself for now. He would tell her when the time was right.

Griffin met Marissa at her doctor's office. He was looking forward to hearing his child's heartbeat for the first time. He had never been so excited about anything.

"We didn't have to drive separate cars," he told her once they were inside the medical building.

Marissa glanced up at him. "I thought we were keeping our relationship quiet for now."

"I am still your mentor, Marissa," Griffin said. "People expect us to spend time together."

"You're here now," she told him. "Let's just focus on the doctor's visit for now. Okay?"

Griffin nodded.

He leaned down and planted a kiss on her lips.

They sat down in the reception area. While they waited, Marissa thumbed through a magazine dedicated to pregnancy.

Griffin reached over and took her hand in his. He held her hand until they were called into the examination room.

Marissa introduced him to her doctor.

When she pulled up her shirt, Griffin eyed the roundness of her belly. Her pregnancy was advancing and soon Marissa would not be able to hide it. The baby seemed to grow overnight.

"Would you like to hear our baby's heartbeat?" Marissa asked him.

Griffin nodded.

When he heard the tiny little heart beating rapidly,

it was the most amazing experience of his life. It was the best feeling in the world, Griffin decided.

Hearing his child's heartbeat really made it a reality for him. He was going to have a beautiful little son or daughter.

Marissa was watching him, as if trying to read into his expression.

Griffin grinned. "That heartbeat is the most beautiful sound I've heard outside of yours."

Her eyes filled with tears. "That's how I felt the first time I heard it."

He leaned down and kissed Marissa's forehead. "Thank you for giving me this beautiful gift."

"Speaking of beautiful gifts," the doctor interjected, "how would you two like to take a peek at your son or daughter?"

"We would love it," Marissa said.

The doctor scheduled the ultrasound and after he pronounced her pregnancy healthy and progressing, they walked out of the doctor's office.

"Can you believe it?" she said. "We get to see our baby in a couple of days."

Griffin wrapped an arm around her. "I can't wait."

"I'm so glad you came with me. I really wanted to share this experience with you, Griff."

"I really want this child," he told her. "I really want our family, Marissa. I'm not going to pressure you about getting married, but I want you to know how much you and this child mean to me."

"I know that we didn't plan for this to happen, Griff."

"No, we didn't," he said. "But I already love this

baby. There's no point in looking back. We need to focus on our future."

"You're right," Marissa said. "I just need to know that you are with me for the long haul. Children need both parents, but if you are not interested or would rather not be a father, I need to know now. I am more than willing to raise my child as a single mother."

"Marissa, I would never let you do that. I am with you, one hundred percent."

Chapter 17

Griffin insisted they ride together for the sonogram appointment. Besides, he knew Marissa was too excited to drive.

"I feel like I'm about to burst," she said when they neared the medical center. "I can't believe how much water I had to drink for this appointment."

"I thought you were trying to float out of the office," Griffin teased.

Marissa gave him a playful punch in the arm.

She shifted in her seat.

"Are you okay?"

She nodded. "I just feel full. I hope the sonogram doesn't take too long, though. I don't want to end up embarrassing myself or you."

Griffin pulled his car into the parking lot of the medical center. He got out of the car and walked around it to open the door for Marissa.

She checked in and they sat down in the waiting room. It seemed to take forever till they were called and the procedure began.

Griffin's eyes were glued to the monitor once the technician sat down and began gliding the wand over her stomach.

"Do you know what you are looking at?" Marissa asked him.

"Huh? What did you say?"

She laughed. "I asked if you knew what you were looking at."

He smiled. "Not yet."

He hoped she knew that he was going to be a great father. He was very attentive to her, even in the office, no matter how much she tried to discourage it. Marissa had told him earlier that she had a feeling her assistant suspected something was going on between them, but Roberta had not said anything to her. Her assistant was not one to spread gossip, so they felt sure that Roberta would keep her suspicions to herself.

Marissa's breath caught in her throat at the first sight of her baby. "There he is," she murmured.

Griffin peered closer. "Honey, I don't think that's a boy."

She met his gaze briefly before returning her attention to the monitor. "We're having a girl?"

They both looked at the technician, who smiled and nodded.

Griffin's eyes filled with happy tears. "A little girl," he whispered. "This is my daughter."

He wiped his eyes with his hands. "We have a daughter, Marissa."

Marissa was crying, as well. "Yes, we do."

Griffin's heart swelled with love for Marissa and his unborn daughter and he silently vowed to protect them both for the rest of his life. For the first time ever, there was something more precious to him than his career.

Marissa and her mother were still not on the very best of terms, but she reluctantly agreed to go shopping with Jeanette and Jillian.

"I love spending time with my girls," Jeanette said as they stepped out of her Mercedes-Benz.

They walked into a boutique located in Society Hill.

Jeanette walked up to a rounder of gowns and pulled one out, saying, "You should try this one on, Marissa. It would look stunning on you and it's perfect for the Christmas party."

"I don't care for it," Marissa said. The dress really was lovely, but it would do nothing to hide her rounded stomach. She needed to find something with a full skirt and high waist.

Jeanette frowned. "You don't like it? This looks like you, dear."

"Mom, I don't want that one."

Marissa glanced over at Jillian, silently pleading for help.

"I don't think that color will look good on her," Jillian stated. "It will wash out her complexion."

Jeanette held the pumpkin-colored gown up to Marissa's face, and then said, "Oh, I see what you mean."

Marissa released a short sigh.

Coming out with them was a huge mistake. She

should have known better than to agree to a day of shopping with her mother. Marissa placed her oversized purse in front of her stomach.

Jillian sent her an amused look.

Marissa spied a dress on the wall and walked over to view it closely.

"That doesn't look like your style at all," Jeanette said from behind her.

"I actually like it," Marissa said, looking over her shoulder at her mother. "I love the emerald-green color."

"Go try it on," Jeanette suggested. "Let's see it on."

"Mom, I'm not in the mood for trying on clothes," Marissa said. "You were the one who wanted to go shopping. You and Jillian shop—I'm just here for support."

"Honey, I've noticed that you've put on a little weight," Jeanette said in a low voice. "Are you still working out?"

Marissa almost choked. "Excuse me?"

"It doesn't look bad on you," her mother quickly assured her. "But if you're not comfortable with it, just exercise and cut back on the junk food."

Jillian walked away and pretended to be admiring a dress.

Marissa did not know how to respond, so she just kept quiet.

"Dear, I did not mean to embarrass you."

"You didn't," she said.

Marissa shifted her purse from one shoulder to the other. She purposely kept it in front of her to hide her stomach.

They left that store a few minutes later and walked to

the next one. As they strolled by the baby store, Marissa's steps slowed.

Jillian sent her a warning look, prompting her to quicken her pace.

Marissa and Jillian both hid their frustration as their mother tried to pick out gowns for them.

"Mom, we're not little girls anymore," Jillian said. "You don't have to pick out our clothes."

Marissa agreed.

Jeanette sighed in exasperation. "You both used to love when we would go shopping for your wardrobe."

"We were what? Ten?" Marissa asked.

"I helped you pick out your dress for prom," Jeanette responded.

"I let you do it because you were paying for it," Marissa confessed. "And for the record, it was not my first or second choice."

"Ditto," Jillian uttered. "We love you, but please stop trying to dress us."

Jeanette sighed. "Oh, all right."

When they arrived home, three hours later, Jacob was in the family room watching television. He pointed to the bags in her mother's hands and said, "Retail therapy?"

Jillian broke into a short laugh. "You can say that. These new shoes I bought have given me a new outlook on life."

Jacob looked at Marissa. "What did you buy?"

"Nothing," she said. "I was just there for support."

He laughed.

Jeanette set her bags down near the back stairs. "Marissa, dear. When are you planning to tell us about this guy you've been seeing?"

Marissa glanced over at Jillian, who shrugged.

"How do you know I've been seeing someone?"

"Well, you have been spending a lot of time away from home lately, and your dad says you are not working late."

"Daddy, are you keeping tabs on me?" Marissa asked.

"Hey, don't use me to avoid answering the question."

"Okay, I have been seeing someone. You will find out who he is very soon, but for now…I'm keeping his identity a secret."

Her mother frowned. "Why? Is there something wrong with him? Is he married?"

"No, he's not married," Marissa replied. "Mother…"

"Then why are you being so secretive?" Jacob wanted to know. "I was about to ask you the same question, but your mom beat me to it."

"I just want to see where the relationship is headed." Without waiting for another question from her parents, she walked up to her room.

Jillian followed her in. "Why don't you just tell them that you and Griff are dating?"

"I don't know," Marissa admitted. "I guess I just need to be sure that we are on the same page this time. I thought we were before and we were not—I don't want to make the same mistake twice."

Jillian shook her head. "I don't get it. I can see as clear as day that Griff is in love with you and that you love him. What are you two waiting for? An engraved invitation to your own wedding?"

"Griff has never said those three little words that I really need to hear. He tells me how much he cares for me, but he has never once said the *L*-word. I won't even consider marriage without love."

"But he shows it to you, Marissa. Think about it. The way he touches you. The way he looks at you. Baby sister, you still have so much to learn."

Jillian headed to the door. "Don't mess around and let him get away. You will regret it for the rest of your life if you do."

Jillian's words echoed in Marissa's mind long after she left.

Two days later, Griffin had a surprise for Marissa.

"What's this?" she asked when he handed her an envelope.

"I know how crazy things have been for you and so I thought that you could use a day of pampering."

Marissa opened the envelope to find a gift card to a local day spa. She read over the brochure and chuckled. "They have a Pregnant Babymoon package. I have never heard of anything like this. How did you know about it?"

"Someone gave my cousin a gift card to the spa at her baby shower. She raved about the place, so I thought you might like it, too."

"This is so sweet of you, Griff."

He moved to stand close to her. "There is nothing too good for the two most important ladies in my life."

"You are spoiling me."

Griffin smiled. "You deserve it. I'll cover your cases

so you don't have to worry about anything. Take the day and just enjoy."

When Griffin left her office, Marissa reviewed the brochure once more. "Spa services for women and moms of all ages, with all services and products available for our moms-to-be," she murmured.

Griffin had been nothing but supportive since she told him about the pregnancy. He was truly a good man and she enjoyed spending time with him. Things were good between them for now, but Marissa still was not totally convinced they had a future together. Griffin wanted to be a father to his child, and she knew that he would sacrifice his own happiness to make that happen. She couldn't—

Jake walked into her office, interrupting her thoughts.

Marissa quickly hid the brochure beneath her legal pad. "What's up?" she asked her brother.

"Have you talked to Harper lately?"

"Why?" she asked cautiously.

"He's been acting strange," Jake said.

Marissa cleared her throat nervously. "Maybe he's just tired. The Morton case is wearing on all of you."

Jake agreed. "I'm taking a nice vacation once this is all over."

She smiled at her brother. "You deserve it. I'm sure your wife will appreciate it, as well."

Their conversation turned back to Harper.

"I tried to talk to him," Jake said, "but you know that Harper and I are like oil and water."

Marissa chuckled. "You two just need to put away the measuring sticks."

He broke into a grin. "All right. I'm going to let you get away with that, Marissa. I'd better get back to my desk. I'm expecting a phone call from Morton."

Marissa got up and walked over to Jillian's office.

Her sister glanced up from her computer monitor. "What's going on?"

She placed the packet on Jillian's desk. "Griff arranged for me to take a day off and spend it at a spa."

Jillian smiled. "That's so sweet."

"This spa is different, Jillian," Marissa said. "It specializes in prenatal spa treatments."

"Really?"

She nodded. "Jillian, he's been so good to me. We have a great time together."

"So, what is the problem?"

"The problem?" Marissa repeated.

Jillian leaned forward in her chair. "Why won't you marry this man if he's so wonderful?"

Marissa met her sister's gaze. "Because Mr. Wonderful has not mentioned that he loves me. I have to make sure that this is just not about the baby."

Their conversation was halted when Jacob and Frank walked into the office.

"How are my two girls?" their father asked.

"Fine," Marissa and Jillian responded in unison.

Frank smiled at Marissa. "I'm hearing good things about you, young lady."

"Thank you," she murmured. "I'm doing my best."

Marissa rose to her feet and quickly excused herself. She was not ready to be anywhere near her uncle. She did not understand why her mother had been unfaithful, but Marissa really did not get how Frank could betray his own flesh and blood—his own brother.

Chapter 18

The media were everywhere.

News vans were parked outside the courthouse and reporters filled the steps, milling around in front and on the side of the building.

Pulling her jacket closed to brave the winter air, Marissa walked with Jillian and her cousin Shawn. They were going to be in court for most of the day to watch the proceedings. Her brothers Anthony and Marcus would come over when they had some time away from their own cases.

Griffin was already in the courtroom with their client, Jake and Harper. Her father and uncle were still at the office, but Marissa was sure they would venture over at some point. Just as they entered the building, Albert Clark appeared behind them.

They entered the courtroom and took their seats.

Griffin glanced at Marissa and she smiled.

"I saw that," Jillian whispered. "So did Marcus and Anthony. You'd better be careful."

"I don't care," Marissa whispered back. "I love Griffin. To be honest, it's really hard to keep my feelings to myself."

"So, what are you two waiting for?"

"I guess for the right moment." Marissa gave her sister a sidelong glace. "I just want to make sure that Griffin feels the same way I do. I know that he cares for me, but I want to know without a doubt that he loves me, Jillian."

Her sister nodded in understanding.

Marissa's eyes traveled to Harper. Her cousin was staring off into space. She was not sure that he was aware of his surroundings. She rose to her feet and went to talk to him.

"Hey, you."

"Marissa, I didn't know you were here."

"I don't think you are aware of anyone—not the way you were just staring off into space."

He looked embarrassed. "I had something on my mind."

"Harper, what can I do for you?"

He smiled at her. "I'll be fine. I've had some tough decisions to make, but I know what I have to do—what's best for me."

It was almost time for the trial to begin, so Marissa quickly returned to her seat.

She noticed Harper lean over and whisper something in Jake's ear before he moved to sit at the end of the table beside Griffin.

Harper had just removed himself as lead attorney. Marissa could hardly believe her eyes.

"What is going on with Harper?" Jillian asked in a low whisper.

"I don't know," Marissa murmured. "Maybe he is not as prepared as he would like to be, so he thinks it's best to remove himself."

Jillian turned to Harper's brother, Shawn. "Do you know what's up?"

"He's been unhappy lately," Shawn said. "He said he was about to make some changes in his life. Maybe this is part of it."

"I don't think it's anything to worry about," Marissa said.

"You and Mom," Jillian said. "Harper and Uncle Frank... What in the world is going on in my family?"

Marissa stiffened in her seat. "What do you mean?"

"You and Mom are at odds and the other night when I was leaving the office, I heard Harper and his dad arguing. Something about living a lie."

She froze. "What else did you hear?"

"That was pretty much it. I didn't stick around to listen, but just the little bit that I heard was pretty intense."

Everyone settled down and the courtroom became silent as the judge made his entrance.

Marissa stole a peek at Griffin, who seemed to be going over his notes. Her gaze traveled to Harper.

He glanced in her direction, his expression bland.

A few seats down, Blaine Morton looked as if he were about to face a firing squad. Marissa almost felt sorry for him.

She was mildly surprised when Griffin gave the opening statement.

Marissa soon realized that it was strategy on her brother's part. Griffin was not a Hamilton and because of his humble background, the jurors would easily identify with him. She had to admit, Griffin was brilliant and engaging.

I love him so much, she thought.

The next day Harper did not show up in court.

Marissa stepped out in the hallway and placed a call to his cell phone. It went to voice mail. "Harper, where are you? You're supposed to be here at court."

She tried Azure next. When she answered, Marissa asked, "Where is Harper?"

"Marissa, he has taken this thing with his father real hard. He needs some time."

"Is he okay?"

"For the most part," Azure said. "I'm sure Harper will give you a call soon."

"I just wanted to make sure he was okay. Thanks, Azure."

Marissa hung up and returned to the courtroom.

"Did you find him?" Jillian asked. "Did you talk to Harper?"

She shook her head.

Jillian gave her a look of disbelief. "What is going on with him? I can't believe he would do something like this—especially now."

Marissa knew that her cousin was having a hard time, but to just not show up for court like this… This was not like Harper.

It was time for the proceedings to begin.

Marissa listened as several victims told their stories of how they had been scammed of their life savings. The stories were heartbreaking.

Griffin was very sympathetic and understanding of their plight.

Marissa could not help feeling a sense of pride as she listened to Griffin. His questions were deliberate, but he did not badger or make the witnesses feel as if they had done anything wrong.

She stayed in court until noon and then returned to her office.

"I was hoping we could have lunch together," Griffin said from the doorway. "You left pretty quickly."

"I needed to get back here," Marissa said. "Have you or Jake spoken to Harper?"

Griffin shook his head. "I left him a voice mail."

"He's still having a hard time with…"

Griffin nodded in understanding. "Sweetheart, how are you holding up?"

"I'm fine. I just feel terrible for Harper."

"He will get through this, Marissa. Both of you will."

"Griff, I hope you're right. Things are better between Mother and me, but I have not really forgiven her yet."

Jacob knocked on her door.

"Daddy?"

"Do you know what's going on with Harper? Shawn doesn't seem to know anything. You and Harper have always been close. Has he said anything to you?"

Griffin excused himself, leaving Marissa and her father alone.

"I haven't talked to him."

"Frank can't seem to catch up with him either. I have never seen Harper just skip out on a trial like this. What's wrong with the boy?"

Marissa could not help wondering how long before Jacob discovered the truth about Jeanette and Frank, and about her and Griffin. He would feel betrayed by all of them—she was sure of it.

What would happen to the firm when all of the secrets came out?

As the case progressed, Marissa found her resolve weakening when it came to Griffin. She loved him deeply.

Would it be so terrible to marry Griff?

Maybe he did not love her now, but the baby had brought them closer together. Marissa was even beginning to think of them as a family. If only she could be positive that he would not come to view them both as a burden.

Later that evening, Marissa and Griffin cuddled on the leather sofa in his living room.

"I'm so proud of you," she told him. "You were wonderful in court today."

"Thank you," he murmured. "I enjoy being able to look over and see you there."

Marissa reached over, took Griffin's hand and laid it on her belly. "Do you feel that?"

His eyes widened in surprise. "Was that a kick?"

She smiled. "I think so. It felt like a little thump."

"It's incredible," he said. He laid his head against her stomach. "Hello, baby girl," he whispered. "What are you doing in there?"

Marissa laughed. "I can't wait to meet her."

He gazed up at her. "Neither can I."

The touch of Griffin's lips on hers was a delicious sensation, and Marissa returned his kisses with reckless abandon.

Marissa breathed lightly between parted lips. She did not say a word, but she was sure that Griffin could see her desire in her gaze.

No words were spoken from their lips; they communicated only through their hearts.

The baby kicked again.

"I guess she doesn't want to feel left out," Marissa said with a grin.

Griffin kissed her stomach. "You will never have to worry about that, little girl. I am going to make sure you and Mommy know just how much I adore you both."

He glanced up at Marissa. "I promise."

Chapter 19

"You're done for the evening?" Griffin inquired when they met in the hallway of the law firm the next night.

Marissa nodded. "Yes, and I have to tell you I'm so glad. I'm tired."

He walked Marissa out of the building and through the parking deck to her car. "It's too bad you're tired," Griffin said. "It's a Friday night and I was thinking about seeing a movie. I thought maybe you could join me?"

Marissa broke into a grin. "Sure. I'm actually in the mood for a movie. I can handle that."

"Great. Do you want to leave your car here and ride with me?"

"I'll follow you. But I need to freshen up a bit," Marissa said. "I'll only be a few minutes. I keep some clothes in my office."

Ten minutes later, Griffin met Marissa at the elevator. She had changed into a pair of jeans and a sapphire-blue sweater paired with silver flats, which complemented the white-gold fashion necklace she wore around her neck.

"Ready?"

She gave a slight nod. "Let's go."

Griffin escorted Marissa to her car and then went to his. She followed him a couple of blocks to the movie theater.

They were shocked when they ran into Roberta and her family.

"Your girls are getting so big," Marissa told her assistant.

She and Roberta talked a few minutes more before going their separate ways.

Marissa surprised Griffin by laughing. "You know we're acting like a couple of nervous kids who have been caught with their hands in the cookie jar."

Griffin chuckled. "You're right."

"We're just two people here to watch a movie," Marissa said. "We have nothing to hide. We are friends…"

He shook his head. "We are more than friends."

She glanced up at him. "You're right."

They were much more than friends, Marissa acknowledged. It was time that she started looking at Griffin in a different way. Things had changed between them—in a way that she had dreamed of from the first moment she had ever laid eyes on Griffin. She was about to enter uncharted territory with this man, and if she was truthful to herself, she was nervous.

She was grateful for the movie and the two hours

of silence and darkness to examine her thoughts and still her nerves.

When they emerged from the theater, Griffin gestured toward the ice-cream parlor in the next block. "Interested?"

"Sure," Marissa answered.

A few minutes later, they sat in one of the booths eating ice cream.

"I'm going to have to do another mile on the treadmill," announced Marissa. "I don't mind, though. I haven't had an ice-cream sundae this good in a while."

"I know exercise is good for you and the baby, but make sure that you are not doing too much."

"I'm not overdoing it. I'm actually in a prenatal fitness class." Marissa checked her watch. "It's getting late. I should probably be getting home."

"Why don't you come home with me?" Griffin suggested.

"As much as I would love that, I can't. I'm not quite ready to take what we have to the next level."

Griffin did not try to convince her otherwise.

They left the ice-cream shop and headed to the parking deck, hand in hand.

Over the weekend, Griffin saw Marissa when he could—in between prepping for the next week of the trial. He hated for the evenings to come to a close but he was glad she'd agreed to have lunch with him Monday.

He knew exactly what he planned to tell her.

"Marissa, I think that it's time we stopped hiding."

Marissa had just sat down in the restaurant and she

looked up to meet his gaze. "What are you saying, exactly?"

"We're together," Griffin said. "We're a couple. Let's act like it." He reached across the table and took her hand in his own. "Are you okay with this?"

Marissa nodded.

"After the charity ball, I would like to tell everyone about the baby," Griffin said. "Hopefully the trial will be over and so will the fundraiser."

"Mother has enough to worry about with the ball," Marissa said.

"There is something that I have been meaning to tell you," he said.

"What is it?"

"Maybe we should order first." He watched her as she looked over her menu.

Marissa gasped. "Griffin…"

"Yes?"

Inside her menu was a section that was titled *Marissa*. She read the wording beneath.

You mean the world to me and I tried to think of a special way to tell you what has been in my heart from the first moment I met you. Marissa, I love you and I want to spend the rest of my life showing you just how much. This menu features all of your favorites plus something special: our wedding feast. Would you please do me the honor of becoming my wife in the very near future?

A waiter walked over to the table carrying a covered tray. He opened it to reveal a small velvet box.

"Will you marry me, Marissa?"

Stunned speechless, she met his gaze.

Griffin opened the ring box to reveal a stunning two-carat cushion-cut emerald flanked by a channel row of diamonds on each side. "I love you."

Marissa wiped away a tear. "I…I never expected… I thought we were just going to have lunch."

"Will you marry me?" Griffin asked a second time.

She nodded. "Yes, I'll marry you."

The dining room exploded in applause.

"This is just the beginning," Griffin told her as he placed the ring on her finger. "I have a very special evening planned for us tonight. We have to celebrate."

"You really know how to surprise a girl," Marissa said with a smile.

Griffin was on top of the world.

He and Marissa were going to be married and he was ecstatic at the idea of having her as a wife. Griffin was looking forward to waking up beside her every day for the rest of their lives.

He was glad they had decided to go public with their romance—it was time.

Marissa was getting larger. She would not be able to keep the pregnancy a secret much longer, despite the loose clothing, jackets and oversized handbags.

She was growing large with his child.

It was an incredible thought.

His assistant walked into his office, bringing him back to the present. When she left a few minutes later, Griffin's thoughts returned to Marissa.

He could hardly wait for the evening to come.

Griffin had ordered a romantic dinner to be served at his apartment. He had also ordered a dozen roses for Marissa.

He wanted Marissa to spend the night with him, but he would not pressure her to do so. She had requested some movies to watch, so he made a mental note to pick them up. However, if Griffin had his way, they would spend the evening making love.

"Were you able to rent the movies I suggested?"

They had just finished a meal of lobster scampi over linguini, grilled vegetables and hot, buttery rolls. For dessert, they shared chocolate-covered strawberries and nonalcoholic champagne.

Griffin burst into a short laugh. "You didn't make a suggestion—you *told* me what you wanted to see."

"You wanted to see them, too," Marissa said as she moved into his open arms.

Griffin held her snugly. "This feels so right to me," he whispered. "I love you so much, sweetheart."

"I love you, too," she whispered.

Marissa buried her face against his throat.

"What's that smile for?" Griffin asked.

"I'm really enjoying myself," she confessed. "This has been a perfect day."

"You sound as if you're surprised."

Marissa pulled away from him. "Not really. I just did not expect things to happen the way that they did." She admired her engagement ring. She had taken it off when she'd returned to the office after lunch, but now she wore it proudly.

Griffin laughed. "So, tomorrow we let everyone in on our secret."

"At least this one won't break up my family," Marissa said in a low voice.

Griffin disappeared off to the kitchen and returned a few minutes later with two bottles of water. He handed one to Marissa, who smiled in gratitude.

His smile stirred something within her. Marissa unscrewed the top of her water and took a quick sip. "I don't know about you, Griffin, but I'm still trying to get used to the idea of us together like this."

Griffin started the DVD, then sat next to her on the sofa, saying, "I've heard pretty good reviews about this film."

The mere touch of Griffin's hand against her own sent a warming shiver through her. She struggled to keep her mind on what he was saying. "I'm not so sure I'm interested in watching any movies tonight."

He glanced over at her.

Their eyes met and held.

Griffin broke the stare by asking, "Are you sure about this?"

Instead of answering him with words, Marissa kissed him in response.

A delicious heat warmed her body and she could barely conceal her desire for him. Griffin reached over, pulling her closer to him. "I find you incredibly beautiful."

When he kissed her again, Marissa's senses reeled as if they short-circuited and made her knees tremble.

Breaking their kiss, Marissa buried her face against Griffin's throat; her trembling limbs clung to him helplessly. She was extremely conscious of where his warm flesh touched her.

Griffin touched a finger to her chin and lifted her head up.

"I never thought I could feel this way about anyone," he confessed. "I tried to fight my feelings for you, but it was a losing battle. I surrender willingly to your love."

His finger brushed against her skin, moving back and forth, making it difficult for Marissa to think.

"Griff, I fell in love with you shortly after we started working together. I just did not think that you felt the same way."

"I have always been told to stay away from workplace romances. When I became your mentor, Albert sat me down and had a long discussion about pursuing anything other than a professional relationship. He warned me to stay away from you."

"Especially since I am the boss's daughter," Marissa stated.

Their gazes locked and each of them could see the desire mirrored in the other's eyes.

Griffin pulled her back into his arms. "Tonight this is just about you and me."

He kissed her again, lingering, savoring every moment.

Marissa's emotions whirled. Blood pounded in her brain, leapt from her heart.

Without another word, Griffin picked her up and carried her into the bedroom.

He undressed her in between kisses.

Marissa wrapped her arms around him. "I love you, Griff."

He stared into her eyes. "I love you, too, sweetheart. More than I can ever put into words."

She stepped away from him, giving him a frontal view of her body. "Then show me," she murmured softly.

Griffin watched Marissa as she slept, his heart overflowing with love. He resisted the urge to pinch himself. Seeing Marissa in his bed seemed almost too good to be true.

I am a very lucky man.

Marissa stirred but did not wake up.

Griffin kissed her lightly on the cheek. She stirred once more, this time moaning softly.

He lay down and placed a protective arm across her waist.

Griffin did not fall asleep right away. He reveled in the way Marissa's body felt against his own. They were a perfect fit. His body responded to the silky feel of her skin against his.

He loved her deeply.

Marissa snuggled against him, igniting a wave of desire within him. They had made love earlier, but he wanted to relive the passion they had shared once more.

Griffin tried to recall if he had ever been as happy as he was now. No woman had ever made him feel the way that Marissa did—no relationship he'd ever had came close to what they shared.

She turned in his arms.

Griffin planted tiny kisses along her cheek and neck in an attempt to wake her up.

Marissa moaned softly but did not open her eyes.

He was not going to give up. Griffin continued his slow seduction.

Her passion aroused, Marissa opened her eyes.

They soon connected in a sensual dance that lovers did, the union igniting fireworks that they both experienced.

Afterward, Griffin continued to hold her close as they slept, satiated from the fulfillment of desire.

Griffin smiled. "I love you, baby." He couldn't stop proclaiming his feelings for her. It was as if a dam of emotion had broken inside him.

She reached over and took his hand in hers. "I love you, too."

Chapter 20

Griffin and Marissa awoke to the news that Houston Douglas had been arrested in Costa Rica and was awaiting extradition.

Stunned, she turned to Griffin. "Did you know anything about this?"

"No, but this is the break we needed," Griffin said as he sprinted out of bed. He picked up his cell phone and placed a call to Jake.

"Turn on your TV," he said when Jake answered on the other end. "Man, you are not going to believe this."

Marissa was careful not to make any noise, as she did not want her brother to know that she had spent the night with Griffin. They were planning to tell her family about their relationship later today.

She padded quietly across the floor to the bathroom. She showered while Griffin and Jake discussed strategy.

He was off the phone when she walked out of the

bathroom wrapped in a towel. "Do you need my help with anything?" she asked.

Griffin kissed her. "We might."

He walked into the bathroom. "I'll be out in a few minutes."

By the time he'd showered, Marissa was dressed.

"I'll head to the office," she told him. "Call me if you need anything. I'll try to come to the courthouse this afternoon."

He pulled her gently into his arms. "Hey, last night was beautiful. I didn't want to let you leave here without my saying that. I love you."

Marissa smiled. "I love you, too, Griff."

When she arrived at the office, the media were out in full force. Houston's arrest was the talk of the town. According to the reports that were coming into the firm, Houston had confessed to being the one who defrauded all of Blaine Morton's clients. He told the feds that Morton had nothing to do with the fraud.

Marissa called Jillian. "Can you come to my office for a minute? I have something to tell you."

She pulled her ring out of her purse and slipped it on her finger.

Her sister showed up a few minutes later. She sat down in a chair and asked, "Where were you last night?"

"I stayed with Griffin."

"Why am I not surprised?" Jillian said with a grin. "I take it that he said the *L*-word."

Marissa held up her hand, displaying the engagement ring. "Yes, he said the *L*-word, but not only that. Griffin proposed and I accepted. We are getting married."

Jillian grinned. "Congratulations. I'm so happy for you."

"We're going to tell Mom and Dad later tonight," Marissa stated. "Not about the engagement just yet, but that we're dating."

"First the news with Houston and now this. It's turning into an interesting day all around."

"Why do you think Houston decided to come forward?" Marissa asked.

"I heard that he has cancer and it's stage four. He wants to come home and be with his family. I guess he figures he's not going to live long enough to go to trial."

"Maybe Morton's trial will end soon."

Jillian agreed. "In view of all that's happened, I'm sure Jake and Griff will ask for a dismissal of all charges against Blaine Morton."

By the time Marissa prepared to leave the office and head over to the courthouse, news came in that Houston would be on a plane that evening. He was returning to the States to face charges.

She and Jillian rushed over to the courthouse to join her brothers.

Griffin, Jake and Blaine Morton were standing on the steps talking with the media.

"It's over," Marissa said.

"The charges have been dropped," Jillian surmised. "We won."

They moved in closer to listen to the press conference.

"Houston Douglas is on a plane right now headed back here to be formally charged. He confessed that he acted alone and that our client is yet another victim," Griffin announced.

Marissa met Griffin's eyes and smiled. She was so proud of him and the way that he handled the media. He was a natural, she decided. He had found his calling.

He smiled back.

After the press conference, she and Jillian joined Griffin and Jake.

"Good job," Jillian told them. "It's too bad that Harper didn't hang around to see this. Does anybody know where he is? I tried calling his cell, but it just goes to voice mail."

Marissa cleared her throat awkwardly. "I think he's taking some much-needed time off. He could be burned out."

The conversation turned back to Blaine Morton.

"I hope that he can find a way to move on with his life now that this is over," Jillian said. "This whole ordeal looks like it's taken its toll on Morton."

"Unfortunately, there is no way to repair the damage that was done to so many of these victims, including Blaine Morton," Griffin said. "From all news accounts, Houston Douglas has been given a death sentence."

When they arrived back at the firm, Jacob ushered the associates into the conference room. Frank and Albert were already seated at the table.

"Good job," Jacob said. "Houston's confession and return only made things easier for us, but we were still victorious. Jake and Griff presented a strong case and I believe we would have won regardless."

Everyone around the table agreed.

After the meeting, Marissa rose to her feet and prepared to leave the room, but Jacob stopped her.

"I noticed that you did not come home last night. You and this young man must be getting pretty serious."

"We are," Griffin said from behind her.

Marissa turned around. "Griff…"

He walked up and stood beside her. "Marissa and I have been seeing each other, sir."

Jacob eyed them both for a moment before smiling. "I had a feeling that it was you, Griff. I've seen the looks you two exchange when you think no one's paying attention."

"Really?" Marissa asked. "Why didn't you say something?"

"I figured you'd tell me when you were ready."

"We wanted to see how things progressed between us," Marissa explained. "Griff was ready to go public earlier, but I wouldn't let him." She did not want to tell her father about their engagement just yet. Marissa wanted her dad to get used to seeing them together first.

She explained this to Griffin when they left the conference room.

"Another secret," he said.

"It's not like that, Griff. I just don't want to spring all of this on them at one time."

"I'm sure they can handle it."

Marissa folded her arms across her chest. "I don't want to argue with you, Griffin. It's been a great day for you and I don't want to ruin it. Can we at least wait until after the charity ball? We will tell them about the baby and our engagement. Okay?"

Griffin gave a reluctant nod.

"Are you mad at me?" Marissa asked.

"No, I'm not. I guess I'm just ready to share our news with the world."

"The ball is only a few days away," Marissa said. "We can tell them the day after. I give you my word."

The associates decided to go out for drinks after the workday ended. They wanted to celebrate.

Griffin and Marissa sat down at a nearby booth.

Jake walked over. "Is there something I should know?" he asked. "You two sure seem cozy."

Marissa met Griffin's gaze and smiled.

"Your sister and I are dating," Griffin announced.

"How long has this been going on?"

"For a while," Griffin responded. "I fell in love with Marissa shortly after we met."

"But we didn't act on our feelings until a few months ago," Marissa contributed. "So yes…we are a couple."

"Does Dad know?"

Marissa glanced up at her brother. "He knows. We told him earlier. Griff and I see no reason to keep our relationship a secret any longer."

"Well, all I'll say is that you had better not hurt my sister."

"I have no intention of ever hurting Marissa."

Several of the associates were dancing to the music. Griffin took her hand in his. "Want to dance?"

Marissa shook her head. "Not right now. I just want to sit right here with you."

When she snuggled in close, Griff asked, "When do you want to get married? Before or after the baby comes?"

"Before," she replied. "I don't want a huge fancy wedding."

"What do you want?"

"Something small. I'd like a very intimate and romantic ceremony."

Marissa noticed that several of their coworkers were watching them from a distance.

Obviously Griffin noticed it, too. "I have a feeling that we are going to be the topic of the watercooler gossip tomorrow," he said.

Marissa nodded in agreement. "You know...we could give them something to really talk about."

He grinned. "What do you have in mind?"

"Kiss me."

Her words brought a smile to his lips.

Griffin did as Marissa requested.

A few of the associates looked shocked, but others did not.

Marcus and Anthony navigated over to the booth. "I guess that kiss was your way of announcing that you two are involved," Marcus said.

"Can't say that I'm real surprised," Anthony told them. "I knew my sister had feelings for you."

It was Marissa's turn to look surprised. "I was that obvious?"

"No," Griffin said. "I wasn't always so sure."

Jillian joined them, saying, "C'mon, let's party. We're supposed to be celebrating."

Marcus took her by the hand. "Let's show them how we do it, sis." They headed to the dance floor.

Griffin and Marissa joined them.

When the song ended, Marissa led him off the dance

floor. They sat down and watched their coworkers laughing and having a good time.

"What do you suppose Blaine Morton is doing right now?" she asked Griffin.

"I don't know. His whole life has changed, so maybe he is trying to pick up the pieces. He wants to try and save his marriage."

Shortly after nine, Marissa and Griffin decided to call it a night.

"Are you coming over?" he asked.

"Not tonight," she said. "I'm sure Daddy's told Mother about us. I think I should go home."

"I'm going to miss holding you in my arms."

She gazed at him lovingly. "Me, too."

After a long kiss good-night, Marissa made her way home.

Jeanette met her practically at the door. "Your father told me about you and Griffin. I think it's wonderful. He's a nice young man and he has a great future with the firm."

"I'm glad you approve, Mother."

"Why were you keeping your relationship a secret? You and Griffin have nothing to hide."

"We just wanted to keep it between us for a while," Marissa explained.

"You have always been so secretive," Jeanette said.

Marissa chewed her bottom lip to keep from responding. Her mother was one to talk—she was keeping an explosive secret.

After a moment, she said, "I'm just private, Mother."

"It wasn't a criticism, dear."

Marissa changed the subject. "Did Daddy tell you what happened today?"

Jeanette smiled. "It's been all over the news, but yes. He told me. I feel so sorry for Blaine. Houston ruined his life, and it looks like he is not going to have to pay for it—at least not on this side of eternity."

Marissa eyed her mother. "Regardless, he will have to answer for his sins. We all have to face the consequences for our actions."

Jeanette glanced away from her daughter. "You are absolutely right about that."

Marissa walked into the kitchen and washed her hands in the sink while her mother retrieved a bottle of water and a piece of fruit out of the refrigerator.

They stayed in the kitchen talking while Marissa prepared a cup of herbal tea.

"So, when did you and Griffin get together?" Jeanette asked.

"Things changed between us about five and a half months ago," Marissa answered, trying to be as honest as she could.

"Really?"

She nodded. "We decided not to rush into anything serious, but just recently that changed, as well. Griff and I love each other, Mother."

Jeanette smiled. "I'm so happy for you."

"Thank you," Marissa murmured. She took a sip of her tea and then asked, "When did you realize that you loved Daddy?"

"The day I met him," Jeanette responded with a smile. "We fell in love so fast—it was a whirlwind romance. His parents didn't want us to rush into marriage, but Jacob did not want to wait." She gave a short laugh. "They actually thought that I was pregnant and that's why we wanted to marry quickly."

Marissa stiffened but kept her expression bland.

"Jacob and I married right away and I became pregnant on our wedding night. Jake was born nine months to the day we married." Jeanette walked over to the breakfast table and sat down.

Marissa followed.

"Before I knew it, there were five of you. Jacob was working all of the time while I was stuck at home. For a time, I started to resent him."

Marissa had never heard her mother talk about this part of her life—not in this way. She wondered if her mother was about to confess her affair. "What happened?"

"Your father and I grew apart for a while, but I loved him so much that I could not give up on our marriage. We talked and made some changes. Once we weathered that storm, your father and I have never once looked back."

"Do you love Daddy now as much as you did when you married him?"

Jeanette gave Marissa a sidelong glance. "I love him even more. Your father is a wonderful man and I am so lucky to be his wife. I wake up each morning giving thanks to have him by my side."

Marissa yawned. "I'm sorry."

Jeanette rose to her feet. "We both have to be up early, so we should probably call it a night. Jillian must still be at the bar."

"That's where I left her," Marissa said.

Upstairs in her room, Marissa readied for bed.

She walked over to the window in her room, letting her gaze drift over the moonlit sky. Philadelphia was beautiful at night.

There was a soft knock on her door.

Jillian stuck her head inside. "It's me. I heard you moving about."

"I guess we were the topic of discussion after we left," Marissa said.

"Nope," Jillian replied. "Harper was the focus of our discussions. Harper and Shawn had lunch earlier."

Marissa was not surprised. After all, they were brothers.

"Harper is no longer with the firm," Jillian announced.

She could hardly believe what she was hearing. "What did you just say?"

"Harper's left the firm. He's decided to start his own office." Jillian sat down on the edge of Marissa's bed. "Jake thinks that it has something to do with him."

"It doesn't," Marissa said.

"How do you know?" Jillian asked. "Do you know what's going on with Harper?"

"I just know that it has nothing to do with Jake."

"Is it Uncle Frank?"

Marissa did not respond.

"I know that they haven't been on the best of terms for a while now," Jillian said. "Shawn says that Uncle Frank is very upset over Harper leaving the firm."

When Jillian left her bedroom, Marissa picked up her phone and called Harper.

"I guess you heard the news," Harper said when he

answered. "I knew I would be hearing from you sooner or later, Marissa."

"How could you leave the firm?"

"How can you stay?" Harper asked her. "I can't stand being around my dad and his hypocrisy."

"I know that you're angry right now, Harper. You just need some time and space from the situation."

"I have that by working for myself," he announced. "You know that you're more than welcome to join me."

"I don't want to leave the firm, Harper."

"And you are okay with working around Frank Hamilton, your real father?"

Marissa was silent.

"I thought so."

"Whoever this person is—I wish he or she had just kept mum about this. I hate what has happened to you and your father. I hate that it's placed a wedge between me and my mother."

"I had to do what was best for me, Marissa."

"I'm going to miss you."

"It's not like we're never going to see each other again," Harper said. "I'm still in Philly. In fact, my office is going to be in Center City, so I'm not that far away. We're family, Marissa."

After they hung up, Marissa considered calling Griffin but decided that it could wait until she saw him the next day.

She was filled with renewed anger at what her mother had done. Marissa wanted to understand how Jeanette must have felt back then, but it still did not give her the right to cheat on her father with his brother.

* * *

Humming softly, Marissa sat down at her desk.

The first thing on her agenda was to check her email. Marissa was expecting an email from a client with some documents she needed to file with the court.

Griffin strode into her office with purpose. "I guess you already know about Harper leaving?"

Marissa nodded.

"Is it because of what happened?" he asked.

"Yes. He does not want anything to do with his father." Marissa still had a hard time thinking of Frank Hamilton as her biological father.

"That's too bad," Griffin muttered. "Your dad just called a staff meeting, so I guess he's about to reassign some of Harper's cases."

She groaned. "Great. Just what I need—more work."

Griffin agreed.

Marissa pushed away from her desk and rose to her feet. "I guess we'd better get in there. Daddy did not seem too thrilled with Harper just up and leaving like that."

"How are you feeling?" Griffin asked.

She smiled at him. "Great, actually."

They walked by Roberta, who grinned and winked at Marissa.

Jacob and Frank were in the conference room talking in low voices.

Marissa chewed on her bottom lip. She hoped that her uncle was not in there confessing his sins. This was not the time or the place for such a conversation.

She cleared her throat noisily as they entered the room and sat at the conference table. She folded the ends of her jacket together to hide the roundness of her growing belly.

Once the other associates and Albert arrived, Jacob closed the door.

Frank glanced around the room and then said, "I'm sure all of you are aware that Harper is no longer an associate here at the firm. He has decided to strike out on his own, and I for one wish him much success."

No one uttered a word.

Jacob poured himself a glass of water before saying, "With Harper gone, we are down one attorney with a heavy caseload. Frank and I will cover his upcoming trial dates through the New Year. The other cases will be divided among all of you."

It was just as Marissa had expected. More work.

She was just about caught up on her own caseload; however, it would not help to complain. They all had to pitch in until another attorney was hired. Albert had just announced that they would soon start looking for Harper's replacement.

After the meeting, Griffin walked Marissa back to her office.

"I'm in court this afternoon," he told her, "but I'll come back here when I'm done. If you're still here, we can grab some dinner."

She gave him a smile. "I'll be here."

When he left for his own office, Roberta walked up to Marissa. "I've been wondering just how long you two were going to walk around this office acting like you weren't in love."

The two shared a laugh and then Marissa went to work. Her day was a busy one. She worked through lunch and around three, she relocated to her sofa, when her back started to ache. She kicked off her shoes and settled back against the cushions, her laptop on her lap.

Griffin found her there when he returned to the office at five-thirty. She was so focused on her work that she almost didn't see him standing there.

"Are you ready to leave?" Griffin asked.

"Yes. I'm hungry." Marissa slipped back into her shoes and rose to her feet.

Griffin took her laptop and placed it on her desk. "Let's get out of here."

He took her by the hand and led her toward the door.

Two days ago, Marissa had surprised Griffin with two tickets to see the Philadelphia Eagles play on Sunday. He invited her to go with him.

She enjoyed watching a football game every now and then, but Marissa was not as huge a fan as Griffin was.

"Thank you," Griffin told her as they took their seats.

Marissa smiled at him. "I know how much you love your Eagles."

He gave her a sidelong glance. "So, what do you think?"

She glanced around the stadium, then down at the field. "Honestly?"

Griffin nodded.

"The Eagles organization needs to pay to get their cheerleaders new outfits." She gave him a pinch on the arm. "They are much too distracting."

He laughed.

Marissa lowered her voice and whispered, "Some of these football fans are pretty trashy. Look at that guy over there. He is so drunk that he has already passed out. He won't see any of this game."

Griffin smiled. "I guess this is what he considers a good time."

The game started.

Marissa found the game riveting—more so than she thought she would. She cheered for every touchdown and got upset with every fumble.

After the game, they went to Griffin's apartment. He had purchased a team jersey for Marissa, and she tried it on for him.

"Thanks for today," Griffin said. "I always enjoy an Eagles game, but today was special. It was nice to be able to share this part of my life with you."

Marissa was touched by his words. "I actually had a good time, as well."

She settled against the cushions of his sofa.

"Hungry?" Griffin asked. "I can make us some sandwiches and a salad. I have some deli meat in the fridge."

"I'll take the salad," Marissa said.

He got up and went into the kitchen.

Marissa stretched out on the sofa. She was tired.

When Griffin returned, he found her fast asleep.

Chapter 21

The next day, Marissa went back to Griffin's apartment with him when they left the office.

She placed a quick call to let her mother know that she would not be coming home that night. "I don't want my parents to worry," she told Griffin.

"I understand. I'm a bit surprised that your father isn't coming after me with a shotgun. I'm sure they know we're sleeping together."

She chuckled. "I have a feeling that my parents try not to think about what we may be doing."

Marissa's eyes traveled around the apartment, taking in the tasteful but sparse furnishings.

"I like the space," Griffin explained. "I didn't want the apartment to look crowded, but don't worry. We are not going to live here after we get married. I'd like for us to start looking for a house."

"This place is nice, Griff," Marissa said. "You have

three bedrooms, so there is enough room for the baby and me." She did not want Griffin to feel pressured about buying a house. Becoming a father and soon-to-be husband was enough to deal with for the moment.

He shook his head. "I want a house for our daughter." Griffin's tone brooked no argument. "She deserves the best that life has for her."

"Okay," Marissa said with a smile. "We'll start looking for a house. I have a friend who is a real-estate agent. We can meet with her sometime next week if you'd like."

"I still can't believe we're here like this," Marissa confessed later as they lay on the floor in front of the fireplace. "This still feels like a dream to me."

Griffin's eyes traveled over her face and then slid downward. "It's very real, sweetheart. When I came to work at the firm, I never expected to meet or fall in love with anyone. I was there to prove myself and make partner one day. I was going to follow Albert Clark's advice to the letter. I wanted to prove that I was just as good as a Hamilton, if not better."

Griffin met her gaze straight-on. "I want you to know that you changed all that for me, Marissa."

The air around them suddenly seemed electrified.

"It was the same for me, Griff. I did not come to the firm looking for a man. I was there to prove that I could be just as good an attorney as the rest of my family. I wanted their respect."

"You've earned it, Marissa. They are all very proud of you."

It pleased her greatly to hear this.

He touched her face. "I never thought I could love anyone as much as I love you."

She awarded him a smile. "Griff, I have waited such a long time to hear those words."

"Why didn't you ever tell me how you felt?" Griffin asked.

"After our first night together...I wanted to tell you, but then you told me that you wanted to keep our relationship strictly professional."

"I'm so sorry for hurting you, Marissa. At the time, I thought I was doing the right thing."

"How do you really feel about it now? Is this the right decision for you, Griff?"

"Yes," he said. "I can't imagine my life without you in it, Marissa."

It took a moment for Marissa to find her voice. "I feel the same way. My heart truly belongs to you, Griff."

Griffin pulled her into his arms, holding her close. He kissed her.

Marissa laid her head against his chest. Whenever she was in his arms, the only way she could define the feeling she got was that it was like coming home.

It felt perfect.

It felt right.

His mouth covered hers once more.

Happiness welled up in Marissa. She could feel her heartbeat racing and desire igniting in her belly. She felt as if she were losing herself in Griffin. It was as if the two of them were becoming one being.

Turning in his arms, Marissa lifted her mouth to him, kissing him softly.

Unnamable sensations ran through her as Griffin's

hands traveled down her body. She felt the heat from their closeness and her body began to burn with his touch.

He gently grasped Marissa's hand, his fingers folding into hers. "I want you to meet my parents," he told her. "Saturday morning. We can tell them about the baby and our engagement. The ball is that night. Then on Sunday, we will tell your parents."

"No more secrets," Marissa murmured. "Well, except the one about my mom's affair. Griff, I really don't know what to do about that situation. I do not want to see my dad get hurt. He loves my mother so much. I believe that she also loves him, but what she did was wrong."

"You and your mother have to talk about this, Marissa. It is the only way you'll find some measure of closure."

She gave a slight shrug. "I don't know, Griff. Maybe I should just let this secret die with me. I just hope that the person who contacted Azure will leave it alone, as well."

"Honey, I don't think you can ever just forget this."

"But I can try to move on," Marissa said. "Harper is so bitter right now. I don't want that to be me. My mother is not perfect, but she is still my mother."

"I will support you in whatever you decide," Griffin stated. "No matter what happens, we will find a way to get through it together."

Griffin introduced Marissa to his parents on Saturday.

"It's very nice to meet you," his mother said with a warm smile.

He sat down beside Marissa and took her hand in his. "There's something we need to tell you both," Griffin said. "Marissa and I are engaged."

"I knew it," his mother said. "I told your daddy that you were planning to get married. I had a feeling when you called and told me you were bringing Marissa to meet us."

"There's more," Griffin told them. "We are also going to have a baby."

"Oh," his parents said in unison.

"I love Marissa with my entire being," Griffin stated. "We are excited about this baby and are looking forward to becoming parents. We plan to get married before the baby comes."

His mother gave him a knowing smile. "I can see how much you love Marissa."

"I guess we had better start picking out names for our grandchild to call us," his father said. "I think I want to be called Paw-Paw."

Marissa felt some of the tension in her body melt away.

Griffin's parents were very sweet and they went out of their way to make sure that she was comfortable. They pulled out photo albums to show Marissa pictures of Griffin as a baby.

By the time they left, around noon, she knew she'd love being part of the Jackson family.

"I thought that went well," she told Griffin during the drive back to Mt. Airy. "Your parents were very sweet, although they did not hide their shock well."

He laughed. "I already know my mother is going to

wear my ear out next week for not preparing her for the news."

"I hope it isn't too bad," she said. "But first, we have to get through telling my parents. I just hope they take it as well as your parents did."

Griffin dropped her off at Integrity.

Marissa went inside to speak to her mother, and then she was on her way again—this time to the hair salon.

She returned home three hours later, with her hair pinned up and her nails freshly painted for the charity ball later on that night.

Her mother was on the phone with the hotel going over some last-minute details.

Marissa waved at her and then quietly made her way upstairs to her bedroom.

Jillian stopped by her bedroom. "I wanted to see what Liz did with your hair."

Marissa turned around slowly. "What do you think?"

"You look beautiful," Jillian complimented. "Pregnancy agrees with you," she added in a low voice.

"Thank you," Marissa said. "We told Griff's parents this morning."

"How did it go?"

"They were shocked, of course, but they congratulated us and they were really nice."

"When are you and Griff telling our parents?" Jillian asked. "You've gotten bigger."

"We're going to tell them tomorrow," Marissa announced. "We can't wait any longer. I just want to get through this charity ball. After tonight, there won't be any more secrets."

* * *

The Hearts and Hands Charity Ball was always a huge affair, with proceeds benefiting the Tuck Me In Foundation, and attended by many of the Who's Who in Philadelphia. Several celebrities had also traveled to attend the event. The media were also well represented.

Jeanette looked stunning in her silver-sequined gown. She moved gracefully around the room, pausing here and there to acknowledge the attendees.

Jeanette and her committee had planned an evening where guests could enjoy a sit-down dinner, silent auction, raffles and dancing. A local band provided music for dancing, while an orchestra provided background music during dinner.

Marissa spotted her mother and walked over to where she was standing. "Mother, everything looks beautiful."

Jeanette smiled. "Thanks, dear."

Frank Hamilton and his wife, Vanessa, made their grand entrance. Marissa noted how exquisite her aunt looked in one of her own designs. The pewter-colored Grecian-style gown complemented her copper-colored skin tone and her dark hair, which flowed to her shoulders.

They glanced in Marissa's and Jeanette's direction but did not join them.

Marissa was glad because the two women had always merely tolerated each other. She also noted that her mother did not quite meet Frank's gaze.

"Is there anything I can do to help you?" she asked Jeanette.

Her mother shook her head. "I think we have everything under control. You go and join Griffin. You two have a good time tonight."

Marissa and Griffin avoided her uncle and aunt as they made their rounds. They paused briefly to talk to her brother Marcus and his date.

"Do you know if Harper is planning to come tonight?" he asked Marissa.

"I don't know," she said. "I haven't talked to him in a while."

"I talked to him about a week ago," Marcus said, "but I forgot to ask him about the ball. I wish I knew what was really going on with him."

"Harper has always wanted his own law office," Jake said, joining them. "He has never really wanted to work in the family firm. He did it to please his father."

Marissa and Griffin excused themselves and continued to work the room. The firm was a major sponsor of the annual event hosted by Jeanette.

"Let's check out the items up for auction," Griffin suggested.

There were Park Hopper passes to Disneyland, tickets to sporting events with prime seating, artwork and gift certificates to five-star hotels and spas. As Marissa looked through the prizes, Griffin pulled her close.

"Have I told you how beautiful you look in that gown?" he asked in a loud whisper.

Marissa looked up at him. "No, it must have slipped your mind."

"You look exquisite."

"Thank you," she murmured. "You look quite handsome yourself."

He leaned down and planted a quick kiss on her lips.

"Enough of that," Jillian said, coming up beside them.

"I love that gown on you," Marissa told her sister. "Red is definitely your color."

Marissa had chosen to wear a cream-colored ball gown with red accents. The full skirt helped to camouflage her pregnancy, although Marissa worried that if someone looked hard enough, her secret would be exposed.

She caught Vanessa staring in their direction.

"Aunt Vanessa is watching us," she told Jillian and Griff. "Do you think she blames us for Harper's leaving the firm?"

"Why would she?" Jillian wanted to know. "Harper is a grown man. He is free to make his own choices."

"But you know how she can be at times," Marissa said. "Whenever something went wrong, she always blamed us. Her children could do no wrong."

Jillian agreed. "Well, she can't blame us for this."

Marissa nodded. Her sister had no idea just how right she was.

They navigated to their assigned tables in preparation for the dinner.

Griffin and Marissa were seated at the same table as her parents along with Jillian and her date for the evening. At the next table, Frank and Vanessa were seated with sons Shawn and Nelson along with their dates. There were two empty chairs for Harper and Azure, if they showed up.

Marissa could not wait for this night to end. All she wanted to do was go back to Griffin's apartment and relax in his arms. She did not want to think about anything other than her future with the man at her side.

After they had eaten, Jacob escorted Marissa to the dance floor.

As they danced, her eyes grew bright with unshed tears. Marissa loved Jacob dearly and it broke her heart to consider that he was not her biological father.

"Honey, why do you look so sad?" Jacob asked. "Things look like they are going well with Griff."

"Griff and I are fine, Daddy."

"Then what is it?"

"I was thinking of all the father-daughter dances you have taken me to. I was always so proud and loved showing you off. You were the most handsome and brilliant of all the fathers there."

Jacob laughed. "I'm sure all of the little girls felt the same way about their fathers."

"But in my case, it was absolutely true."

"My baby girl, I want you to know that I am very proud of all you have accomplished. I have to confess that I never thought you would follow the rest of the family into law, but you did, and it suits you."

"I have always wanted to make you proud of me, Daddy."

"You have," Jacob confirmed.

"Daddy, how do you really feel about Griff and me being involved?" Marissa inquired.

"I like Griff," he said. "I can see that he makes you happy."

"He does."

The music stopped and Jacob was about to escort

Marissa back to her seat. Suddenly she knew what she had to do. She stopped in her tracks, saying, "Daddy, I have to tell you something."

Chapter 22

"What is it, Marissa?"

She glanced over at her mother and then back at her father. She couldn't do it. "I just wanted to tell you how much I love you, Daddy. I feel very lucky to have you in my life."

Her father gave her a hug. "Baby girl, I love you, too."

Marissa returned to her seat.

"You okay?" Griffin asked in a low whisper.

"I almost told him about the affair."

"What stopped you?" Griffin asked.

"My love for him," Marissa answered. "I love him too much to destroy him like that. This secret is going to die with me, Griff. I am going to do whatever is in my power to make sure Daddy never finds out the truth."

"What about your mother?"

Marissa's eyes traveled the ballroom in search of

Jeanette. She found her mother standing near the stage surrounded by the media.

"It will take time, but hopefully, I will be able to forgive her one day."

Griffin covered her hand with his own. "We have so much to look forward to, sweetheart."

Marissa smiled and nodded. "Yes, we do."

"Jacob is your father and nothing will ever change that," Griffin said. "Biology has nothing to do with it."

"I know what you're saying, Griff. Jacob has been my father in every way that matters."

Griffin leaned closer to her and whispered, "Do you know if Frank knows you are his daughter?"

"I don't think so," she said.

Marissa stole a peek over at the next table. She met her aunt's gaze and gave a tiny smile, which Vanessa did not return. "Harper did not mention it to him and Uncle Frank did not bring it up."

She could still feel her aunt's eyes on her, making her uncomfortable.

What's going on with Aunt Vanessa? she wondered.

Jeanette spent most of the evening on her feet, greeting guests and granting interviews. Marissa and the rest of her family joined her for a series of pictures that would be featured in the society section of the newspaper.

They looked like the perfect family.

They were anything but, Marissa silently acknowledged.

Marissa felt the hairs on the back of her neck stand up as she returned to her seat. She glanced around.

Vanessa boldly surveyed her from head to toe. Holding her head in a haughty manner, she met Marissa's gaze and smiled. The look was not one of warmth.

Did she know about the affair? Marissa wondered.

No, she couldn't know. Harper would never have told his mother about the affair.

Marissa's attention shifted back to her mother. It was almost time for her to acknowledge the sponsors.

Jacob escorted his wife to the stage.

He attempted to leave, but Jeanette grabbed his hand and gazed lovingly at him.

With Jacob at her side, Jeanette began her acknowledgment. "This year's event has been another successful campaign, thanks to the generosity of our donors," she began. "We raised more than two million dollars this year."

Applause thundered throughout the room.

Marissa smiled. Her mother's work had paid off.

As happy as she was for her mother, she felt the need to get out of that ballroom and get some fresh air.

"Do you mind if we go outside for a few minutes?" she asked Griffin.

He rose to his feet and together, they left the ballroom. They stood outside on a paved patio aglow with delicate white lights.

"Your mother certainly looks in her element," he said.

"Yes, she does," Marissa agreed.

"I never knew that this kind of life existed outside of television when I was growing up," Griffin confessed. "I definitely never thought I would be attending something like this. I didn't know it was possible until I met Albert."

"Is that why you're so focused on being successful?" Marissa asked.

Griffin nodded. "I grew up with my father working two jobs. He was never able to attend any of my games. My mother worked and in the evenings, she would help my grandmother with her sewing. She worked in alterations for a dry cleaner."

"I guess you think I'm just a spoiled little rich girl."

"I did when I first met you," Griffin confessed. "I thought the same about your brothers and sister. I felt the same way about your cousins. Even most of the people I went to college with. I had no one to pay my way—I went to college on a basketball scholarship and worked to win more."

Marissa smiled. "Your determination certainly paid off."

"It did," Griffin agreed.

She turned to face him. "You have never shared this part of your life with me."

"I guess I wanted to tell you that I was wrong about my initial impression of you. Marissa, you have worked just as hard as I have. I know how much you want to prove yourself to your father." Griffin took her hand in his. "Sweetheart, your father is so proud of you. You don't have to try so hard."

"I guess you think I need to just relax."

Griffin smiled. "Yes. Honey, you are a great attorney. Just believe in yourself."

He kissed her. "Are you ready to go back inside?"

Marissa nodded.

"I'm going to get a drink," Griffin announced when they returned to the ballroom. "Would you like something?"

"A Sprite," she said. "Thanks."

Jeanette was the only one at the table when she resumed her seat. Her mother was staring at her, prompting Marissa to ask, "Is something wrong?"

"You have really put on weight."

"Mother, you've always told me that I needed to gain because I looked too skinny."

Jeanette's eyes traveled from her face downward. She took a closer look and uttered, "Oh my God. You're pregnant!"

Chapter 23

"Please keep your voice down, Mother," Marissa hissed.

"What in the world were you thinking?" Jeanette demanded. She waved her hand back and forth, fanning. "You have your whole future to think about, but clearly you weren't thinking at all."

"How dare you!" Marissa uttered. She couldn't hide her anger at the way her mother was talking to her. She was not some teenage girl in high school.

"I suppose Griff is the father."

She could tell that Jeanette was clearly not pleased about the baby. "Of course he is the father of my child. I don't sleep around, Mother."

"How far along are you?"

"I'm twenty-two weeks."

Jeanette shook her head. "I don't understand, Marissa. How could you let this happen?"

Marissa felt under attack. She searched for Griffin but found him across the room, engaged in a conversation with her father.

"You do realize how this is going to look to everyone," Jeanette was saying. "I get it now. The only reason you told us about Griffin was that you were pregnant."

"My relationship with Griff was really not anybody's business."

"I am your mother," Jeanette stated. "How could you keep something like this from me, of all people?" She shook her head. "I've really had enough of your secrets, Marissa. This is just scandalous, not only for us but for the law firm."

"Oh, you're one to talk, Mother," she snapped in response. "What about your secrets?"

Jeanette sent her a sharp look. "I don't know what you're talking about, Marissa. I have no secrets. That was always your department."

"Really?" Marissa said smoothly. "Then what about you and Uncle Frank?"

Jeanette gasped in surprise.

"Griff and I are both single and we love each other," Marissa pointed out. "But you…you were married and you had an affair with your husband's brother. Tell me something, Mother. How could you do that to Daddy? How could you do that to *me?*"

"Nooo…" Jeanette moaned.

Marissa rose to her feet and walked briskly away from the table.

She swallowed hard, fighting back tears.

Throwing a tantrum would not help her now. She

just needed to find someplace private so that she could compose herself.

Her mother had some nerve judging her.

Griffin spied Marissa rushing out of the ballroom. He ended his conversation with Jacob and followed her.

He found her in the hallway standing near one of the windows, staring out.

"Honey, what's wrong?" he asked.

She turned to face him and Griffin could see that Marissa had been crying. "Did something happen between you and your mother?"

"She knows about the baby," Marissa said. "She had the nerve to talk to me about what this would do to our family."

Griffin wrapped an arm around her. "Your mother is just upset right now—probably because she found out about the baby before you had a chance to tell her."

"You should have seen the way she looked at me, Griff. She acted like I had committed a horrible wrong to this family."

"It's the shock talking."

"I don't care," Marissa uttered. "Mother had no right to speak to me that way. I am a grown woman—not some kid in high school." She released a short sigh. "I just want to get out of here. Can we go to your apartment?"

Griffin nodded. "We will go anywhere you want to go, sweetheart."

Just as they were about to walk through the nearest exit, Jeanette called out Marissa's name.

She turned around slowly. "This is not the time or place for this discussion, Mother."

"Marissa, we need to talk about this." Jeanette glanced over at Griffin. "Alone."

She boldly met her mother's gaze. "Griffin knows everything, Mother. Whatever you have to say you can say in front of him."

Jeanette looked humiliated. "Can we please find someplace to talk?"

Marissa pointed to some chairs nearby.

Once they sat down, Jeanette began to explain. "What happened between Frank and me… Marissa, it happened a long time ago."

"It never should have happened," Marissa stated coldly. "You were both married."

"Why don't you just hear your mother out?" Griffin suggested gently.

"Fine," Marissa uttered. "I'm listening."

"I was lonely," Jeanette explained. "I had four children under the age of five. Your father was so busy with work and back then, he was rarely home. There were days when he slept at the firm—he wouldn't even come home. I felt like a single mother."

Marissa eyed her mother but did not respond.

Jeanette continued. "Frank was also very lonely. Vanessa's clothing line was just taking off and she spent most of her time in Europe. Frank and I have always been friends. We were both frustrated and we would vent to each other. Frank understood what I was going through. We were just a source of support for each other."

"When did the affair begin?" Marissa asked.

"There was no affair," Jeanette answered. "It was one night. Jacob and I had had a bad fight and I was upset. Frank and Vanessa weren't getting along either—in fact, he was considering a divorce. Anyway, he came over to cheer me up and…"

"But how could you not tell me that Uncle Frank is my father? Don't you think Daddy and I have a right to know the truth?"

"Is that what you think?" Jeanette questioned. "Heavens, no, dear. Do you honestly think I would lie about something like *that?*"

Marissa glanced over at Griffin, then said, "Even good people keep secrets at times."

"Jacob is your father, Marissa. This is without question."

At that moment, an official from the gala walked over to where they were sitting and said, "Mrs. Hamilton, someone would like to speak to you."

Jeanette gave Marissa one last look before saying, "We will finish this conversation later at home."

"Let's go, Griff."

"You still want to leave?"

Marissa nodded. "I heard her out, but it really doesn't change anything. I'm sure that she desperately wants Daddy to be my real father, but she is obviously in denial."

"She seems convinced that Jacob is your father," Griffin interjected. "Maybe you should finish that conversation."

Marissa shook her head. "It won't matter. I just want

to go back to your place and take a hot bath, then go to bed. With any luck, I'll forget this night ever happened."

Griffin planted a kiss on her forehead. "I don't think that's going to happen, sweetheart."

"But we can try, can't we?"

Before Griffin could respond, the door to the ballroom opened and they could hear a commotion of some sort.

"What is going on in there?" Marissa asked.

"It's your mother," Griffin announced. "She and Vanessa Bonnard are arguing."

Marissa was alarmed. "We need to get over there." Taking Griffin's hand, she practically ran into the ballroom. Her aunt had her mother cornered.

"Who do you think you are?" Vanessa hissed at Jeanette, her eyes filled with anger. "How dare you try and run to my husband every time you have a problem with your family. You don't think I know what is really going on?"

Jeanette's mouth opened in surprise. "What are you talking about?"

"Oh, please," Vanessa uttered. "I am not stupid, Jeanette. I know all about you and Frank. I've known for years."

Marissa gasped and clung to Griffin. "Nooo…"

Her family was falling apart all around her, and Marissa felt as if it was all her fault. She never should have confronted her mother like that.

Griffin wrapped a protective arm around her.

In front of her, the battle between the two women raged on. "Vanessa, can we please finish this conversation someplace private?" Jeanette asked. She looked as if she was about to break down into tears at any moment.

Marissa felt sorry for her mother. She also felt guilty over her actions. She had never wanted to humiliate Jeanette.

She stepped up to them. "Aunt Vanessa," she said. "Don't do this here."

"Why not?" her aunt demanded. "People should know the truth about this family and especially your mother. She has gotten off scot-free for all these years. Everyone thinks that she is such a devoted wife and mother." Vanessa glared at Jeanette. "She is nothing more than a home wrecker."

"That is enough," Jillian muttered as she joined them. "Aunt Vanessa, if you have so much to say, save it for tomorrow. We can talk this out at Integrity."

"Oh no, this place is perfect," Vanessa cooed. "Right here in front of everyone Jeanette cares about. I do not intend to let her escape what she deserves most. Public disgrace."

Marissa eyed her aunt. Vanessa's face was contorted with anger. Instantly she knew. "It was you."

Vanessa glared at her. "What are you talking about?"

"You are the anonymous person who tried to tip off *Eminence* magazine about the affair."

A crowd began to form around them, including Harper.

"What is going on here?" he demanded.

Marissa looked at him, asking, "When did you get here?"

"Just now," he said.

His wife walked up and stood beside him. "Why

don't we take this outside?" she suggested. "The room next door is empty."

Jeanette met Vanessa's angry gaze and said, "I'm sorry."

"Your apology isn't enough," she said.

Frank and Jacob navigated through the crowd, shocked and concerned looks on their faces.

"What is the meaning of this?" Jacob wanted to know.

Frank grabbed his wife by the arm. "What have you done, Vanessa?"

"Let's take this into the other room," Azure suggested again. "Go ahead. I'll stay here and try to salvage this night."

Vanessa laughed harshly.

Azure met her mother-in-law's gaze. "I can't believe you would do this to your own family."

"What do you know about family?" Vanessa snapped. She snatched her arm away from Frank and walked toward the exit.

Azure glanced over at Jeanette and said, "I never told my boss anything about the tip. I will do everything in my power to keep this from coming out."

Jeanette appeared defeated. "Vanessa will only go to another magazine or newspaper. She's made it pretty clear that she wants to destroy me."

Jacob embraced her. "Let's go outside."

Marissa and Griffin followed her parents.

Outside the room, Frank and Vanessa were engaged in an intense argument. He grabbed her and practically pushed her into the empty room next door.

"Let go of me."

Jeanette glanced up at Jacob. "I need to talk to her."

"Mother…" Marissa began. She did not think that Vanessa was ready to listen to anything her mother had to say. It was probably better to wait until things cooled down a bit. "I think you need to give Aunt Vanessa some time."

Jeanette shook her head. "The truth is finally out and I might as well face my past."

They went to the room that Frank and Vanessa had just entered.

Vanessa was irate when Jeanette approached her. "Get away from me," she spat out.

"No. Vanessa, you started this and we are going to finish the conversation. I want you to know that I am really sorry about everything."

Vanessa slapped her. "Frank has made a mockery of our marriage. All of you have looked down your noses at me for years. Jeanette, you had the nerve to judge me for choosing to have a career instead of staying home to raise my children. Then you seduce my husband. You have some nerve."

"You're right," Jeanette admitted. "I was wrong."

Frank turned Vanessa to face him. "I am the one to blame for all of this. You should be angry at me."

She glared at him. "Oh, I am very angry with you."

Their conversation came to a brief halt when Jillian and her brothers burst into the room, followed by their cousins.

"Perfect timing," Vanessa said with a smile that did not reach her eyes. "It's time you all knew the truth about our family."

"Mom, don't do this," Harper pleaded.

"You're right, son," she said. "I think Jeanette should be the one to tell everyone the truth."

"Mom, what's going on?" Marcus asked.

"Since we are having a truth moment, why don't you tell everyone about Marissa?" Vanessa goaded in a loud voice, her arms folded across her chest.

Suddenly all eyes were on Marissa.

Jeanette shook her head. "Leave my daughter out of this."

Marissa glanced up at Griffin and then back at Vanessa. "It's all right, Mother," she said. "It's time for the truth."

Chapter 24

"I agree," Griffin stated. "It's time that everyone learned the truth."

"I'm pregnant," Marissa announced. "Griff and I are having a baby. We should have told everyone sooner, but we just wanted to take some time to get used to the idea ourselves."

Her family congratulated them—all except Vanessa. She stood there glowering at Marissa.

"Anyone with eyes could see that you were pregnant," she uttered. "I've known for months now. Perhaps if your mother hadn't been so busy focusing on her charity ball, she would have known it, as well."

"How can you be so sure she didn't know?" Marissa asked.

"Because she would have died of embarrassment," Vanessa responded. "Her precious little girl...her love—"

"Vanessa and I are calling it a night," Frank said, interrupting her. "Congratulations on the baby."

"Oh, don't think that I am done with this," Vanessa warned. She tried to snatch her arm away from Frank, but he kept a tight grip on her. "You are going to pay dearly, Jeanette."

Marissa sent Griffin a look of gratitude. This was not the way they had wanted to announce the news, but she did not want to risk Vanessa blurting out that Frank was her real father.

The room suddenly grew silent.

Jeanette turned toward Marissa. "For what it's worth, your father knows all about Frank and me. We worked through it and he forgave me years ago."

"It was hard news to hear," Jacob confirmed. "But until then, I had no idea just how unhappy your mom was. When we found out she was pregnant, Jeanette insisted that we know whether I was the father. I loved your mother so much that I was willing to love her unborn child regardless."

Marissa's eyes filled with tears.

He walked over to his daughter and said, "Marissa, you are my child. Frank is not your father."

"We had a paternity test done," Jeanette stated. "I had to know the truth."

Marissa sagged with relief.

Shocked at the turn of events, her siblings just stood there staring at their parents.

Jeanette walked over to Marissa. "I'm so sorry for my behavior."

"We should finish this at home," Jacob stated as he

put his arm around his wife. "For now, we need to walk back into that fundraiser with our heads held high."

Jeanette wiped away her tears. "I have made such a mess of things."

Marissa embraced her. "We will get through this together, Mother."

As soon as they entered the ballroom, Griffin walked up to the stage and grabbed the microphone. Once he had the attention of the attendees, he said, "Honey, I wasn't planning on doing this just now, but I guess the cat is out of the bag."

Puzzled, Marissa glanced at her mother.

"What's going on?" Jeanette asked.

"I don't know."

Griffin pointed to Marissa. "This beautiful, talented woman has made me the happiest man on earth," Griffin announced. "She has agreed to marry me!"

The room burst into applause.

Jacob glanced at his daughter. "Is this true? Are you and Griff getting married?"

"Yes," she said. "Daddy, there is so much we have to talk about."

He nodded in agreement. "But for now, let's just enjoy the rest of this evening."

"I hope you're not mad at me for announcing our engagement like this," Griffin said when he walked off the stage and over to her. "I thought we needed to put some type of positive spin on the evening."

Marissa smiled. "I think you should kiss me. People are watching us."

Griffin did as she suggested.

When she stepped back, Marissa turned to her mother. "Mother, I'm sorry."

Jeanette reached out and took her hand. "Dear, you have nothing to apologize for. What happened tonight was all my doing."

"You were honest with Daddy. Uncle Frank should have been the same with Aunt Vanessa."

"I should be the one apologizing to you," her mother said. "I was horrible to you about the baby. Marissa, I want you to know that I am going to love this baby as much as I love all of my children."

"I know that, Mother."

"I only want the best for you, Marissa. It's all I have ever wanted for any of my children."

"Griffin loves me and I love him."

Jeanette smiled. "I can see that. He is a good man."

"Are you going to be okay?" Marissa asked.

"She's going to be fine," Jacob said as he walked up behind them. "Your mother is a strong woman and she will not break from this." He went to his wife and kissed her. "Like we have done everything else, we will get through this as a family."

After rounds of congratulations, Marissa and Griffin left the gala and drove to his apartment.

"This has been a crazy night," Marissa said when they entered the living room. "I don't know if I could have made it through without you, Griff."

"Your aunt has so much anger and bitterness rooted within. I almost feel sorry for your uncle."

Marissa gave a sad shake of her head. "I have no idea what will happen between them now. Uncle Frank did not seem happy with her at all. I just hope they don't kill each other."

"I'm going to run you a hot bath," Griffin told her. "Then I'm going to give you a massage."

Marissa broke into a grin. "I'd like that very much."

Her cell phone rang when Griffin went into the bathroom, and she answered it.

Marissa frowned. "I wasn't able to speak to you before I left," Vanessa stated. "You know, I used to think that you were such a smart girl, Marissa."

"Aunt Vanessa, what is this about?"

"Has it ever occurred to you that Griffin will do whatever he can to ensure that he makes partner? Including marrying the boss's daughter."

"I know that you're upset right now—"

"I'm actually more concerned about you. Like I said earlier, I knew you were pregnant weeks ago. Griffin is a very handsome and intelligent young man. He may care for you, Marissa, but I'm sure that he cares more for that huge corner office across from your father's."

Marissa did not want to hear any more. "I have to go."

"I just don't want to see you get hurt. After all, you are my stepdaughter. I don't blame you for your mother and Frank's actions."

"I am not Uncle Frank's daughter," she snapped in anger. "Mother had a paternity test done that proves it."

Vanessa was quiet.

Griffin strolled back into the living room and began to gently massage her shoulders while she talked on the phone. "You have a right to be angry, Aunt Vanessa, but you do not have to try and ruin my life or my mother's."

"Harper made the right choice when he decided to leave Hamilton, Hamilton and Clark. You might want to consider doing the same. I'm sure that's the last thing Griffin wants you to do. If he loves you as much as you believe, it won't matter to him." Vanessa said her piece and hung up.

Marissa put away her phone.

"What's wrong?" Griffin asked.

"Nothing," she said.

Marissa studied Griffin's face. Her aunt was wrong about him. She had to be.

"What are you thinking about?"

"Griff, I'm sorry," Marissa said. "I think that I should just go home."

He looked puzzled by her decision. "Are you okay?"

She nodded. "I just… Tonight was really crazy and I just want to go home and sleep in my own bed. Do you mind taking me home?"

"No," he murmured. "Of course not."

Vanessa's words gave Marissa much to think about and she wanted to do it with a clear head—something she would not have while lying in Griffin's arms.

"Jillian, can we talk?" Marissa asked when she entered her sister's bedroom.

"Sure," her sister responded, sitting up in bed. "Why didn't you tell me about Mom and Uncle Frank?"

"I didn't want to believe it myself."

"How long have you known about them?" Jillian asked.

"For a while. Harper came to me when Azure received the tip from Aunt Vanessa."

"Is that why he left the firm?"

Marissa nodded.

"Aunt Vanessa called me when I was at Griffin's apartment," she said. "She wants me to believe that Griffin is only marrying me to make partner."

Jillian shook her head. "I don't believe that, and you shouldn't either."

"As soon as he found out that I was pregnant, he decided we should get married. Jillian, we hadn't even been on a real date. *Who does that?*"

"Sounds to me that you and Griff need to sit down and really discuss this. Marissa, if you have any doubts whatsoever, then it's best to get them ironed out now."

Marissa nodded. "I have to know without a doubt that Griffin wants me because he loves me and not because I am a Hamilton."

The next morning, Griffin strode into her office with purpose.

"I called you last night."

Marissa met his gaze. "I know."

Griffin sat down in one of the chairs facing her. "Did I do something to upset you, Marissa?"

"I've been doing a lot of thinking, Griff. When I told you I was pregnant, you immediately decided that we should get married. We went from having a professional relationship to suddenly considering marriage. It happened so fast."

"What are you getting at?" Griffin asked. "Is there a question somewhere in there?"

Marissa met his gaze. "I want to make sure that we

are doing the right thing, Griff. Having a baby is not a good reason to get married."

"How did we get back to this?" Griffin wanted to know. "What's going on, Marissa?"

"What would you say if I told you that I wanted to leave the firm and go work with Harper?"

"I would say that it's a bad idea."

"Really? Why?"

"Why would you want to leave Hamilton, Hamilton and Clark? Your family built that firm from the ground up. It's your legacy."

Marissa silently noted how worked up Griffin seemed at the idea of her leaving the firm. She had no intention of doing so, but his reaction bothered her.

"What is this really about?" Griffin demanded.

"I don't think we should rush into a marriage," she stated.

"I see."

"I'm sorry, Griff. I got so caught up in worrying about what my parents would think. I just don't think I'm ready for marriage."

He was watching her. "What is it that you're not telling me? I know you well enough to know that you're hiding something."

"Aunt Vanessa called me last night," Marissa said. "You were in the bathroom running a bath for me."

"I gathered that's who you were talking to," he responded. "What did she say?"

Marissa inhaled deeply and then exhaled slowly. "She told me that you only wanted to marry me to ensure that you make partner."

His eyes flashed angrily. "And you believed *her?*"

"I just wanted to be sure, Griff."

"Do you really think that I would be so deceitful?"

Marissa had never seen Griffin so angry since she had known him. "It's not that I believed her. I just thought that maybe we should slow down."

He shook his head. "Marissa, I realize that you are the youngest in your family and they tend to baby you, but I had always thought of you as a grown woman." Griffin paused a moment before adding, "Apparently, I was wrong."

His words stung her.

"Griff…"

He rose to his feet. "You do not have to worry. The engagement is off. I will provide for my child—you will never have to worry about that."

Griffin walked out of the room before she could utter a response.

"Hey, I just saw Griff and he looked upset," Jillian said when she entered Marissa's office.

"He just broke up with me," she announced.

Jillian look stunned. "I'm so sorry."

"Griff was angry with me," Marissa said, "but he was hurt more than anything." She released a long sigh. "Jillian, I think I just messed up badly."

"Why don't you go to him?" Jillian suggested.

"Maybe this is for the best."

Jillian eyed her sister. "Do you really believe that?"

Marissa gave a slight shrug. "I honestly don't know what to believe anymore."

Griffin sat at his desk, baffled.

How could Marissa believe her aunt after everything they had been through in the past months?

Vanessa Bonnard did not know him at all. They had only been around each other a couple of times. Griffin could not understand how Marissa could consider anything that woman said, especially after everything she had done to try to ruin the family.

He wanted no part of these games.

Griffin meant what he had said about his child. He would never neglect the child he'd created with Marissa. He intended to be very involved in his daughter's life.

For the rest of the day, Griffin avoided Marissa and the rest of her family as much as he could. He had enough work to keep himself busy.

That evening, Griffin decided to leave early. It was a rare occasion for him to quit working at five, but today he needed to get as far away from the firm as he could.

Marissa was in the parking garage when he walked out.

"I was just about to come looking for you," she said. "I would like to finish our conversation."

Griffin eyed her for a moment before saying, "There is nothing left for us to discuss. You made it perfectly clear that you think I'll do anything to make partner. As far as I'm concerned, it's pretty clear that you don't know me at all."

"Griffin, I'd really like to sit down and talk."

Griffin shook his head. "If it concerns the child, we can talk. Anything else—I'm not interested."

Marissa looked hurt by his words, but he did not care. "Enjoy the rest of your evening," Griffin told her.

He walked over to his car and drove away before he changed his mind and went back to Marissa. He loved her dearly and it hurt being apart from her, but without trust, there could be no future.

Marissa wiped away her tears.

She could not believe she had allowed her aunt to plant doubts in her mind about Griffin. She should have known better.

Was it too late for them now?

Marissa picked up the gift-wrapped package that sat on the chaise in her bedroom. It was a Christmas present for Griffin. "I'm so sorry, little one," she whispered tearfully. "I really messed things up with your father."

She loved Griffin with her whole heart.

He had shown Marissa love by his faith in her—the way that he looked at her, and the way he made love to her. How could she so easily doubt his true feelings for her?

"I am not going to let your daddy get away this easily," Marissa whispered. "He loves me and I have to trust that love." She picked up her purse. "Let's go see your daddy."

The road was slippery, thanks to an ice event that was not forecasted, but Marissa drove slowly. Along the way she practiced what she was going to say to Griffin.

She was stopped at a red light a couple of streets away from Griffin's apartment when her car was hit from behind by another vehicle.

"Marissa…" someone yelled.

She looked around. It was Griffin.

"Honey, are you okay?" he asked, running up to her car.

Marissa tried to open her door, but Griffin would not

let her. "No, stay inside," he told her. "It's too slippery and I don't want you to fall."

The driver of the car that hit her approached them. "I'm so sorry. I skidded on the ice. Are you okay?"

She nodded. "I'm fine."

They exchanged insurance information while waiting for the police to arrive.

Griffin refused to let Marissa out of the car. He tried to convince her to be checked out at a hospital, but she refused. "It's just a little fender bender," she told him. "My car hardly got scratched."

When they finally made it to Griffin's apartment, he made Marissa settle down on the sofa.

"Were you coming to see me?" he asked.

Marissa nodded. "I owe you a huge apology, Griff. I don't know what I was thinking—I wish I could blame it on hormones, but I can't. You have always been there for me. When you found out I was pregnant, you stepped up."

She met his wary gaze. "I know without a doubt that you love me, Griff. If you give me another chance, I promise I will not ever doubt that love again."

"I want to believe you."

"You can," Marissa assured him. "You're right. I need to grow up and trust my own mind. You've been telling me to do that since I started at the firm. Griff, I love you so much and I will prove that I am worthy of your love."

Their eyes met and held in the tense silence.

"Please say something," Marissa pleaded. "Please tell me that we still have a chance. I want to be with you, Griff. I want to be your wife."

"Marissa, I am in this for eternity. If you're not sure, then we can just be friends and coparent."

She shook her head. "That's not what I want, Griff. It's not what I want for our daughter."

"Are you sure?"

Marissa took his hand in hers. "I am very sure. I want to spend the rest of my life with you, Griff."

"If you want to leave the firm, then I'll go wherever you go," Griffin told her. "But leave because it is something you want to do—not because of me."

Marissa smiled. "I love you so much."

He kissed her on the lips. "I love you, too."

She placed a hand on his face. "Remember that massage you promised me? I could really use one now."

Griffin grinned as he gently massaged her shoulders. "Are you sure that you weren't injured in the accident?"

"I wasn't," Marissa said. "I—"

He was instantly alarmed. "What is it?"

Marissa took Griffin's hand and placed it over the swell of her belly.

"She's kicking," he said in awe. "She's got a strong kick, too."

"She certainly does," Marissa agreed.

"I might have to buy you a football, little girl."

Marissa laughed. "Men and their footballs…"

Later that evening, they lay in bed together.

Griffin stroked her arm softly. "Hungry?"

She nodded. "Starved."

Griffin reached for the phone and sat up in bed. He ordered a sausage, pepperoni and mushroom pizza for delivery. It was Marissa's favorite.

They showered together and got dressed.

"You are so good to me," Marissa told Griffin.

"I intend to take care of you for the rest of my life, sweetheart," he said with a tender smile.

"You're going to the firm's Christmas party this weekend?" she asked. It was always the unofficial kick-off to the holiday season.

Griffin nodded. "Do you think your aunt will be there?"

"She might, but I don't care. Aunt Vanessa can choose to forgive or she can continue to harbor bitterness—I'm just not going to let her pull me back into her drama." It had almost cost her Griffin. Marissa would never allow her aunt to influence her again.

"Good for you," Griffin said. "We need to focus on our future."

Marissa could not agree more. "I really don't know why I believed Aunt Vanessa in the first place. I should have trusted you."

"She strikes me as someone who can be very convincing when she needs to be."

"Griffin, I was wrong for not believing in your love for me. I'm really sorry."

He kissed her. "Honey, I understand. Going forward, I want you to talk to me before you just assume the worst."

"Hopefully, we won't have another issue like this," Marissa said. "Especially since you're going to be my husband."

"Your husband," Griffin repeated. "I love the sound of that."

Marissa followed Griffin out onto the dance floor.

The annual Christmas party was something that the associates and other employees looked forward to each year.

"Your mother really does know how to throw a nice party."

Marissa looked up at him. "If you really want to see a party, just wait until our wedding. Mother wants to hire an orchestra and a harpist for the ceremony."

Griffin smiled. "I thought we were going to have something small and simple."

"That was before we told my parents."

He laughed.

"You know…we can always just elope."

"We're getting married in a week. I do not want to be on your mother's bad side by whisking you away and eloping."

Marissa sighed. "I guess you're right. She has pulled out all the stops and called in a few favors to get this done in such a short time."

When the song ended, they found a quiet table and sat down side by side.

"Griffin, I can't tell you enough how grateful I am to have you in my life. Our little girl is so lucky to have you as a father."

He took her hand in his. "Marissa, I love you so much. What matters to you also matters to me. We're going to make a great team, don't you think?"

Marissa smiled. "Yes, I do."

She gazed at him lovingly. Marissa gave his hand a gentle squeeze. "I trust you, Griffin. I never should have doubted your love for me."

"Marissa, I need you to know that you will always own my heart," Griffin told her.

"And you will always own mine," she said.

Without a word, Griffin pulled Marissa into his arms, touching his lips to hers.

Her kisses would last him an eternity, he decided. There would never be another woman who would make him feel the way he did around Marissa.

Epilogue

Marissa stepped around a bag stuffed with Christmas ornaments.

"Put this one up there," she told Griffin. They were decorating their first Christmas tree as husband and wife. They had only been married for a week.

She handed him another one.

Marissa glanced down at her belly. She was visibly pregnant and Griffin refused to allow her to stand up on the stool to finish the tree. He had taken over for her.

Although it could be irritating at times, Marissa loved that Griffin was so protective of her and the baby. He made her feel safe and secure.

She glanced around the room. The floor was scattered with shopping bags—presents for both her family and his. Marissa and Griffin would be spending Christmas Eve with his parents, and then they would all join her family for dinner at Integrity on Christmas Day.

"It was nice of your parents to invite mine to dinner."

Marissa agreed. "I really love your mother. She is so sweet."

Griffin nodded. "She has a mean streak in her, though—don't let her fool you. She was the disciplinarian in our family."

"Really?" Marissa found that hard to believe.

"Harper looks really happy," Griffin said.

"I noticed it, too," she said. "That's probably because he's convinced Cameron Childs to leave us and sign with him. I'm wondering if Ben and Shawn will leave Hamilton, Hamilton and Clark, as well."

"Childs was Jake's client," Griffin announced as he stepped down off the footstool.

"I know and my brother is not happy about this at all."

"I hope that those two will learn to put aside all the competition," Griffin said. "Family is more important than anything else in the world. Maybe one day they will learn that."

"Maybe it will happen once the babies start coming," Marissa said. "Our little girl definitely changed our lives. As for the firm—we will survive no matter what."

Griffin picked up the shopping bags and arranged them neatly in a corner of the apartment.

"Daddy told me that he and Albert had a conversation about you. Albert wants to place you on the leadership track."

Griffin glanced over at his wife. "Really?"

She nodded. "I'm proud of you."

"It hasn't happened yet. Let's not get our hopes up."

"My dad has a lot of respect for you, Griff. You'll make partner in no time."

Griffin sat down beside Marissa. "You know, all I ever wanted was to make partner, but then I started thinking about what your parents went through. The long hours and young children—I'm not so sure I want that right now. I would rather come home to you and our little girl. I want to read her stories and attend all of her recitals. I don't want to miss any of the important events in any of our children's lives."

"Daddy did not make any of my recitals when I was growing up," Marissa said. "He missed a lot of the boys' games and Jillian's cheerleading competitions. We just understood that he was busy. I do remember being angry with him at times, but it never lasted. Daddy always made us feel loved whenever he was home."

"I don't want that for our daughter. I intend to be present for everything."

Marissa smiled. "I love you for this, but you have worked very hard, Griff. You deserve to make partner one day."

"And one day I will. I'm just not sure I want it anytime soon. My parents worked all the time and I just don't want our daughter to look at me in that way. I want her to know that I will be there whenever she needs me or wants me."

"You are such a wonderful man, Griff."

He kissed her. "You bring out the best in me, Marissa."

Griffin glanced around the apartment. "Hopefully we will find the perfect house before the baby comes."

"Honey, there is nothing wrong with this apartment."

Marissa kissed his hand. "Didn't you tell me to just take it one day at a time?"

He smiled.

"We will take it one day at a time, Griff. You and I have the rest of our lives together, and wherever we choose to live it will have plenty of love inside. This is what matters most."

Marissa lay back in Griffin's arms.

Things were finally back to normal in her family. Frank and Vanessa had come to the wedding, but left after the ceremony. So far, Vanessa had not followed through on exposing her husband's affair with Jeanette. Marissa's mother and father's relationship seemed solid; in fact, they actually seemed closer than ever.

She pointed to a little bag near the tree. "What's that?"

"That's a gift for our daughter."

Marissa sat up. "What did you buy, Griff?"

He stood up and crossed the room, picking up the bag. He brought it to Marissa, who laughed when she saw what was in it.

She held up a tiny Philadelphia Eagles jersey. "Men and their football," Marissa uttered with a chuckle.

"She's going to love football as much as I do," Griffin said. "You'll see."

* * * * *

**A brand-new miniseries
featuring fan-favorite authors!**

THE HAMILTONS 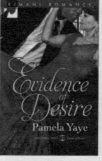 *Laws of Love*

Family. Justice. Passion.

Ann Christopher	Pamela Yaye	Jacquelin Thomas
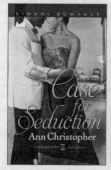	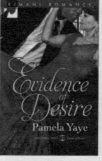	
Available September 2012	*Available October 2012*	*Available November 2012*

REQUEST YOUR FREE BOOKS!

2 FREE NOVELS PLUS 2 FREE GIFTS!

KIMANI™ ROMANCE

Love's ultimate destination!

KROM11B